# *Child of God*

CORMAC MCCARTHY is the author of ten acclaimed
novels, most recently *The Road*. Among his honours are the
Pulitzer Prize for Fiction and the PEN/Saul Bellow Award
for lifetime achievement in American literature.

# CORMAC McCARTHY

*Child of God*

PICADOR

First published 1973 by Random House, Inc., New York

First published in Great Britain 1975 by Chatto & Windus

First published by Picador 1989

This edition first published 2010 by Picador
an imprint of Pan Macmillan, a division of Macmillan Publishers Limited
Pan Macmillan, 20 New Wharf Road, London N1 9RR
Basingstoke and Oxford
Associated companies throughout the world
www.macmillan.com

ISBN 978-0-330-51095-0

3 5 7 9 8 6 4 2

A CIP catalogue record for this book is available from
the British Library.

Typeset by SetSystems Ltd, Saffron Walden, Essex
Printed in the UK by CPI Mackays, Chatham ME5 8TD

# Child of God

I

THEY CAME like a caravan of carnival folk up through the swales of broomstraw and across the hill in the morning sun, the truck rocking and pitching in the ruts and the musicians on chairs in the truckbed teetering and tuning their instruments, the fat man with guitar grinning and gesturing to others in a car behind and bending to give a note to the fiddler who turned a fiddlepeg and listened with a wrinkled face. They passed under flowering appletrees and passed a log crib chinked with orange mud and forded a branch and came in sight of an aged clapboard house that stood in blue shade under the wall of the mountain. Beyond it stood a barn. One of the men in the truck bonged on the cab roof with his fist and the truck came to a halt. Cars and trucks came on through the weeds in the yard, people afoot.

To watch these things issuing from the otherwise mute pastoral morning is a man at the barn door. He is small, unclean, unshaven. He moves in the dry chaff among the dust and slats of sunlight with a constrained truculence.

Saxon and Celtic bloods. A child of God much like yourself perhaps. Wasps pass through the laddered light from the barnslats in a succession of strobic moments, gold and trembling between black and black, like fireflies in the serried upper gloom. The man stands straddlelegged, has made in the dark humus a darker pool wherein swirls a pale foam with bits of straw. Buttoning his jeans he moves along the barn wall, himself fiddlebacked with light, a petty annoyance flickering across the wallward eye.

Standing in the forebay door he blinks. Behind him there is a rope hanging from the loft. His thinly bristled jaw knots and slacks as if he were chewing but he is not chewing. His eyes are almost shut against the sun and through the thin and blueveined lids you can see the eyeballs moving, watching. A man in a blue suit gesturing from the truckbed. A lemonade stand going up. The musicians striking up a country reel and the yard filling up with people and the loudspeaker making a few first squawks.

All right now let's get everbody up here and get registered for ye free silver dollars. Right up here. That's the way. How you little lady? Well all right. Yessir. All right now. Jessie? Have you got it . . . ? All right now. Jess and them is got the house open for them that wants to see inside. That's all right. We're fixin to have some music here in just a minute and we want to get everbody registered fore we have the drawins. Yessir? What's that? Yessir, that's right. That's right everbody, we will bid on the tracts and then we'll have a chance to bid on the whole. They's both sides of the road now, it goes plumb across the creek to them big timbers on the other side yonder. Yessir. We'll get into that directly.

Bowing, pointing, smiling. The microphone in one hand. Among the pines on the ridge the sound of the auctioneer's voice echoed muted, redundant. An illusion of multiple voices, a ghost chorus among old ruins.

Now they's good timber up here too. Real good timber. It's been cut over fifteen twenty year ago and so maybe it ain't big timber yet, but looky here. While you're a laying down there in your bed at night this timber is up here growin. Yessir. And I mean that sincerely. They is real future in this property. As much future as you'll find any-wheres in this valley. Maybe more. Friends, they is no limit to the possibilities on a piece of property like this. I'd buy it myself if I had any more money. And I believe you all know that ever penny I own is in real estate. And ever one I've made has been from real estate. If I had a million dollars I would have it ever cent invested in real estate within ninety days. And you all know that. They ain't no way for it to go but up. A piece of land like this here I sincere believe will give ye ten percent on your investment. And maybe more. Maybe as high as twenty percent. Your money down here in this bank won't do that for ye and you all know that. There is no sounder investment than property. Land. You all know that a dollar won't buy what it used to buy. A dollar might not be worth but fifty cents a year from now. And you all know that. But real estate is goin up, up, up.

Friends, six year ago when my uncle bought the Prater

place down here everbody tried to talk him out of it. He give nineteen-five for that farm. Said I know what I'm a doin. And you all know what happent down there. Yessir. Sold for thirty-eight thousand. A piece of land like this . . . Now it needs some improvin. It's rough. Yes it is. But friends you can double your money on it. A piece of real estate, and particular in this valley, is the soundest investment you can make. Sound as a dollar. And I'm very sincere when I say that.

In the pines the voices chanted a lost litany. Then they stopped. A murmur went through the crowd. The auctioneer had handed over the microphone to another man. The other man said: Holler at the sheriff yonder, C B.

The auctioneer waved his hand at him and bent to the man standing in front of him. Small man, ill-shaven, now holding a rifle.

What do you want, Lester?

I done told ye. I want you to get your goddamn ass off my property. And take these fools with ye.

Watch your mouth, Lester. They's ladies present.

I don't give a fuck who's present.

It ain't your property.

The hell it ain't.

You done been locked up once over this. I guess you want to go again. The high sheriff is standin right over yonder.

I don't give a good goddamn where the high sheriff is at. I want you sons of bitches off of my goddamned property. You hear?

The auctioneer was squatting on the tailboard of the truck. He looked down at his shoes, plucked idly at a piece of dried mud in the welt. When he looked back up at the man with the rifle he was smiling. He said: Lester, you don't get a grip on yourself they goin to put you in a rubber room.

The man took a step backward, the rifle in one hand. He was almost crouching and he held his free hand out with the fingers spread toward the crowd as if to hold them back. Get down off that truck, he hissed.

The man on the truck spat and squinted at him. What you aim to do, Lester, shoot me? I didn't take your place off of ye. County done that. I was just hired as auctioneer.

Get off that truck.

Behind him the musicians looked like compositions in porcelain from an old county fair shooting gallery.

He's crazy, C B.

C B said: You want to shoot me, Lester, you can shoot me where I'm at. I ain't going nowheres for you.

LESTER BALLARD never could hold his head right after that. It must of thowed his neck out someway or another. I didn't see Buster hit him but I seen him layin on the ground. I was with the sheriff. He was layin flat on the ground lookin up at everbody with his eyes crossed and this awful pump-knot on his head. He just laid there and he was bleedin at the ears. Buster was still standin there holdin the axe. They took him on in the county car and C B went on with the auction like nothin never had happent but he did say that it caused some folks not to bid that otherwise would of, which may of been what Lester set out at, I don't know. John Greer was from up in Grainger County. Not sayin nothin against him but he was.

FRED KIRBY was squatting in his front yard next to the watertap where he used to sit all the time when Ballard came by. Ballard stood in the road and looked up at him. He said: Hey Fred.

Kirby lifted his hand and nodded. Come up, Lester, he said.

Ballard came to the edge of the cutbank and looked up to where Kirby was sitting. He said: You got any whiskey?

Might have some.

Why don't you let me have a jar.

Kirby stood up. Ballard said: I can pay ye next week on it. Kirby squatted back down again.

I can pay ye tomorrow, Ballard said.

Kirby turned his head to one side and gripped his nose between his thumb and forefinger and sneezed a gout of yellow snot into the grass and wiped his fingers on the knee of his jeans. He looked out over the fields. I cain't do it, Lester, he said.

Ballard half turned to see what he was looking at out there but there was nothing but the same mountains. He shifted his feet and reached into his pocket. You want to trade it out? he said.

Might do. What ye got?

Got this here pocketknife.

Let's see it.

Ballard opened the knife and pitched it up the bank at Kirby. It stuck up in the ground near his shoe. Kirby looked at it a minute and then reached down and got it and wiped the blade on his knee and looked at the name on it. He closed it and opened it again and he pared a thin peeling from the sole of his shoe. All right, he said.

He stood up and put the knife in his pocket and crossed the road toward the creek.

Ballard watched him scout along the edge of the field, kicking at the bushes and honeysuckle. Once or twice he looked back. Ballard was watching off toward the blue hills.

After a while Kirby came back but he didn't have any whiskey. He handed Ballard his knife back. I cain't find it, he said.

Cain't find it?

No.

Well shit fire.

I'll hunt some more later on. I think I was drunk when I hid it.

Where'd ye hide it at?

I don't know. I thought I could go straight to it but I must not of put it where I thought it was.

Well goddamn.

If I cain't find it I'll get some more.

Ballard put the knife in his pocket and turned and went back up the road.

ALL THAT REMAINED OF the outhouse were a few soft shards of planking grown with a virid moss and lying collapsed in a shallow hole where weeds sprouted in outsized mutations. Ballard passed by and went behind the barn where he trod a clearing in the clumps of jimson and nightshade and squatted and shat. A bird sang among the hot and dusty bracken. Bird flew. He wiped himself with a stick and rose and pulled his trousers up from the ground. Already green flies clambered over his dark and lumpy stool. He buttoned his trousers and went back to the house.

This house had two rooms. Each room two windows. Looking out the back there was a solid wall of weeds high as the house eaves. In the front was a porch and more weeds. From the road a quarter mile off travelers could see the gray shake roof and the chimney, nothing more. Ballard trampled a path through the weeds to the back door. A hornetnest hung from the corner of the porch and he knocked it down. The hornets came out one by one and flew away. Ballard went inside and with a piece of cardboard swept the floor. He swept up the old newspapers and he swept out the dried dung of foxes and possums and he swept out bits of brick-colored mud fallen from the board ceiling with their black husks of pupae. He closed the window. The one pane left tilted soundlessly from the dry sash and fell into his hands. He set it on the sill.

In the hearth lay a pile of bricks and mortarclay. Half an iron firedog. He threw the bricks out and swept up the clay and on his hands and shinbones craned his neck to see up the chimney. In the patch of rheumy light a spider hung. A rank odor of earth and old woodsmoke. He wadded newspapers and set them in the hearth and lit them. They burned slowly. Small flames sputtered and ate their way along the rims, and edges. The papers blackened and curled and shivered and the spider descended by a thread and came to rest clutching itself on the ashy floor of the hearth.

Late in the afternoon a small thin mattress of stained ticking forded the brake toward the cabin. It was hinged over the head and shoulders of Lester Ballard whose muffled curses at the bullbriers and blackberries reached no ear.

When he got to the cabin he pitched the mattress off onto the floor. A frame of dust plumed from under and rolled out along the cupped floorboards and subsided. Ballard raised the front of his shirt and wiped the sweat from his face and from his head. He looked half crazy.

By dark he had all he owned about him in the barren room and he had lit a lamp and set it in the middle of the floor and he was sitting crosslegged before it. He was holding a coathanger skewered with sliced potatoes over the lamp-chimney. When they were nearly black he slid them off the wire with his knife onto a plate and speared one up and blew on it and bit into it. He sat with his mouth open sucking air in and out, the piece of potato cradled on his lower teeth. He cursed the potato for being hot while he chewed it. It was raw in the middle, tasted of coaloil.

When he had eaten the potato he rolled himself a cigarette and lit it over the quaking cone of gas at the rim of the lampchimney and sat there sucking in the smoke and letting it curl from his lip, his nostrils, idly tapping the ash with his little finger into his trouser-cuff. He spread the newspapers he had gathered and muttered over them, his lips forming the words. Old news of folks long dead, events forgotten, ads for patent medicine and livestock for sale. He smoked the cigarette down until it was just a burnt nubbin in his fingers, until it was ash. He turned down the lamp until just the faintest orange glow tinged the lower bowl of the chimney and he shucked out of his brogans and his trousers and shirt and lay back on the mattress naked save for his socks. Hunters had stripped most of the boards from the inside walls for firewood and from the bare lintel above the window hung part of the belly and tail of a blacksnake. Ballard sat up and turned up the lamp again. He rose and reached and prodded the pale blue underside of the snake with his finger. It shot forward and dropped to the floor with a thud and rifled over the boards like ink running in a gutter and was out the door and gone. Ballard sat back down on the mattress and turned the lamp down again and lay back. He could hear mosquitoes droning toward him in the hot silence. He lay there listening. After a while he turned over on his stomach. And after a while he got up and got the rifle from where it stood by the fireplace and laid it on the floor alongside the mattress and stretched out again. He was very thirsty. In the night he dreamt streams of ice black mountain water, lying there on his back with his mouth open like a dead man.

I REMEMBER one thing he done one time. I was raised with him over in the tenth. I was ahead of him in school. He lost a softball down off the road that rolled down into this field about . . . it was way off down in a bunch of briers and stuff and he told this boy, this Finney boy, told him to go and get it. Finney boy was some bit younger'n him. Told him, said: Go get that softball. Finney boy wouldn't do it. Lester walked up to him and said: You better go get that ball. Finney boy said he wasn't about to do it and Lester told him one more time, said: You don't get off down in there and get me that ball I'm goin to bust you in the mouth. That Finney boy was scared but he faced up to him, told him he hadn't thowed it off down in there. Well, we was standin there, the way you will. Ballard could of let it go. He seen the boy wasn't goin to do what he ast him. He just stood there a minute and then he punched him in the face. Blood flew out of the Finney boy's nose and he set down in the road. Just for a minute and then he got up. Somebody give him a kerchief and he put it to his nose. It was all swoll up and bleedin. The Finney boy just looked at Lester Ballard and went on up the road. I felt, I felt . . . I don't know what it was. We just felt real bad. I never liked Lester Ballard from that day. I never liked him much before that. He never done nothin to me.

BALLARD LAY IN the night damp with his heart hammering against the earth. He was watching a parked car through the sparse pale of leaning weeds that rimmed the Frog Mountain turnaround. Inside the car a cigarette flared and lapsed and a latenight D J commented with mindless chatter on the seduction in the rear seat. A beercan clattered in the gravel. A mockingbird that had been singing stopped.

He came from the roadside ducked in a loping run, a shadow that washed up against the cold dusty hindfender of the automobile. His breath was shallow, his eyes wide, his ears pricked to sort the voices from the ones on the radio. A girl said Bobby. Then she said it again.

Ballard had his ear to the quarterpanel. The car began to rock gently. He raised himself up and chanced one eye at the windowcorner. A pair of white legs sprawled embracing a shade, a dark incubus that humped in a dream of slaverous lust.

It's a nigger, whispered Ballard.

O Bobby, O god, said the girl.

Ballard, unbuttoned, spent himself on the fender.

O shit, said the girl.

On buckling knees the watcher watched. The mockingbird began.

A nigger, said Ballard.

But it was not a black face that loomed in the window, that looked so enormous there behind the glass. For a moment they were face to face and then Ballard dropped to the ground, his heart pounding. The radio music ended in a muted click and did not start again. The door opened on the far side of the car.

Ballard, a misplaced and loveless simian shape scuttling across the turnaround as he had come, over the clay and thin gravel and the flattened beercans and papers and rotting condoms.

You better run, you son of a bitch.

The voice washed against the mountain and came back lost and threatless. Then there was nothing but silence and the rich bloom of honeysuckle on the black midsummer night air. The car started. The lights came on and swung around the circle and went down the road.

I DON'T KNOW. They say he never was right after his daddy killed hisself. They was just the one boy. The mother had run off, I don't know where to nor who with. Me and Cecil Edwards was the ones cut him down. He come in the store and told it like you'd tell it was rainin out. We went up there and walked in the barn and I seen his feet hangin. We just cut him down, let him fall in the floor. Just like cuttin down meat. He stood there and watched, never said nothin. He was about nine or ten year old at the time. The old man's eyes was run out on stems like a crawfish and his tongue blacker'n a chow dog's. I wisht if a man wanted to hang hisself he'd do it with poison or somethin so folks wouldn't have to see such a thing as that.

He didn't look so pretty hisself when Greer got done with him.

No. But I don't mind honest blood. I'd rather to see that than eyeballs hangin out and such.

I'll tell ye what old Gresham done when his wife died

and how crazy he was. They buried her up here at Sixmile and the preacher he said a few words and then he called on Gresham, ast him did he want to say a few words fore they thowed the dirt over her and old Gresham he stood up, had his hat in his hand and all. Stood up there and sung the chickenshit blues. The chickenshit blues. No, I don't know the words to it but he did and he sung em ever one fore he set back down again. But he wasn't a patch on Lester Ballard for crazy.

WERE THERE darker provinces of night he would have found them. Lying with his fingers plugged in the bores of his ears against the strident cheeping of the myriad black crickets with which he kept household in the barren cabin. One night on his pallet while half asleep he heard something scamper through the room and vault ghostly (he saw, struggling erect) through the open window. He sat there looking after it but it was gone. He could hear foxhounds in full cry, tortured wails and yelps nigh unto agony coming up the creek, up the valley. They flooded into the cabin yard in a pandemonium of soprano howls and crashing brush. Ballard standing naked saw by palest starlight the front door fill from floorsill up with bawling dogs. They hung there for a moment in a pulsing frame of piebald fur and then bowed through and filled the room, circled once with rising volume dog on dog and then swept out the window howl on howl carrying first the muntins, then the sash, leaving a square and naked hole in the wall and a ringing in his ear. While he stood there cursing two more dogs came through the door. He kicked one as it passed and stove his bare toes on its bony rump. He was hopping about on one foot shrieking when a final hound entered the room. He fell upon it and seized its hind leg. It set up a piteous howling. Ballard flailed blindly at it with his fist, great drumlike thumps that echoed in the near empty room among the desperate oaths and wailings.

GOING UP A track of a road through the quarry woods where all about lay enormous blocks and tablets of stone weathered gray and grown with deep green moss, toppled monoliths among the trees and vines like traces of an older race of man. This rainy summer day. He passed a dark lake of silent jade where the moss walls rose sheer and plumb and a small blue bird sat slant upon a guywire in the void.

Ballard leveled the rifle at the bird but something of an old foreboding made him hold. Mayhaps the bird felt it too. It flew. Small. Tiny. Gone. The woods were filled with silence. Ballard let the hammer down with the ball of his thumb and wearing the rifle on his neck like a yoke with his hands dangling over barrel and buttstock he went up the quarry road. The mud packed with tins trod flat, with broken glass. The bushes strewn with refuse. Yonder through the woods a roof and smoke from a chimney. He came into a clearing where two cars lay upturned at either side of the road like wrecked sentinels and he went past great levees of junk and garbage toward the shack at the edge of the dump. An assortment of cats taking the weak sun watched him go. Ballard pointed the rifle at a large mottled tom and said bang. The cat looked at him without interest. It seemed to think him not too bright. Ballard spat on it and it immediately wiped the spittle from its head with a heavy forepaw and set about washing the spot. Ballard went on up the path through the trash and carparts.

The dumpkeeper had spawned nine daughters and named them out of an old medical dictionary gleaned from the rubbish he picked. These gangling progeny with black hair hanging from their armpits now sat idle and wide-eyed day after day in chairs and crates about the little yard cleared out of the tips while their harried dam called them one by one to help with chores and one by one they shrugged or blinked their sluggard lids. Urethra, Cerebella, Hernia Sue. They moved like cats and like cats in heat attracted surrounding swains to their midden until the old man used to go out at night and fire a shotgun at random just to clear the air. He could'nt tell which was the oldest or what age and he didn't know whether they should go out with boys or not. Like cats they sensed his lack of resolution. They were coming and going all hours in all manner of degenerate cars, a dissolute carousel of rotting sedans and niggerized convertibles with bluedot taillamps and chrome horns and foxtails and giant dice or dashboard demons of spurious fur. All patched up out of parts and lowslung and bumping over the ruts. Filled with old lanky country boys with long cocks and big feet.

They fell pregnant one by one. He beat them. The wife cried and cried. There were three births that summer. The house was filling up, both rooms, the trailer. People were sleeping everywhere. One brought home what she said was a husband but he only stayed a day or two and they never saw him again. The twelve year old began to swell. The air grew close. Grew rank and fetid. He found a pile of rags in a corner. Small lumps of yellow shit wrapped up and laid by. One day in the woods and kudzu jungles on the far side of the dump he came across two figures humping away. He watched from behind a tree until he recognized one of his girls. He tried to creep up on them but the boy was wary and leaped up and was away through the woods hauling up his breeches as he went. The old man began to beat the girl with the stick he carried. She grabbed it. He overbalanced. They sprawled together in the leaves. Hot fishy reek of her freshened loins. Her peach drawers hung from a bush. The air about him grew electric. Next thing he knew his overalls were about his knees and he was mounting her. Daddy quit, she said. Daddy. Oooh.

Did he dump a load in you?

No.

He pulled it out and gripped it and squirted his jissom on her thigh. Goddamn you, he said. He rose and heisted up his overalls and lumbered off toward the dump like a bear.

Then there was Ballard. He'd come up the path with his narroweyed and studied indifference and the rifle in his hand or on his shoulders or he'd sit with the old man in the

28

bloated sofa in the yard drinking with him from a halfgallon jar of popskull whiskey and passing a raw potato back and forth for a chaser while the younger girls peeped and giggled from the shack. He had eyes for a long blonde flatshanked daughter that used to sit with her legs propped so that you could see her drawers. She laughed all the time. He'd never seen her in a pair of shoes but she had a different colored pair of drawers for every day of the week and black ones on Saturday.

When Ballard came past the trailer this very one was hanging up wash. There was a man with her sitting on a fifty gallon drum and he turned and squinted at Ballard and spoke to him. The girl pursed her lips at him and winked and then threw back her head and laughed wildly. Ballard grinned, tapping the riflebarrel against the side of his leg.

What say, jellybean, she said.

What you laughin at?

What you lookin at?

Why, he's lookin at them there nice titties for one thing, said the man on the drum.

You want to see em.

Sure, said Ballard.

Gimme a quarter.

I ain't got one.

She laughed.

He stood there grinning.

How much you got?

I got a dime.

Well go borry two and a half cents and you can see one of em.

Just let me owe ye, said Ballard.

Say you want to blow me? the girl said.

I said owe, said Ballard, flushing.

The man on the drum slapped his knee. Watch out, he said. What you got that Lester can see for a dime?

He's done looked a halfdollar's worth now.

Shoot. I ain't seen nothin.

You don't need to see nothin, she said, bending and picking up a wet piece of cloth from the dishpan and shaking it out, Ballard trying to see down the neck of her dress. She raised up. Just make your peter hard, she said, turning her back and laughing again that sudden half crazy laugh.

Why a cat couldn't bite it now, could it, Lester?

I ain't got time to mess with you all, the girl said, turning back with a grin and picking up the pan. She cocked her hip and set the pan on it and looked at them. Beyond the little trailer the old man walked against the sky rolling a tire and a ropy column of foul black smoke rose from a burning slagheap of old rubber. Shit, she said. If you'ns ever got any of this you never would be satisfied again.

They watched her saunter up the hill toward the house. I'd like to chance it, the man said. Wouldn't you, Lester?

Ballard said that he would.

THE CONGREGATION AT Sixmile Church would turn all together like a cast of puppets at the opening of the door behind them any time after services had started. When Ballard came in with his hat in his hand and shut the door and sat alone on the rear bench they turned back more slowly. A windy riffle of whispers went among them. The preacher stopped. To justify the silence he poured himself a glass of water from the pitcher on the pulpit and drank and set the glass back and wiped his mouth.

Brethren, he went on, a biblical babbling to Ballard who read the notices on the board at the back of the church. This week's offering. Last week's offering. Six dollars and seventy-four cents. The numbers in attendance. A woodpecker hammered at a drainpipe outside and those strung heads listed and turned to the bird for silence. Ballard had a cold and snuffled loudly through the service but nobody expected he would stop if God himself looked back askance so no one looked.

IN LATE SUMMER there were bass in the creek. Ballard went from pool to pool on the downsun side peering through the bushes. He'd been on a diet of stolen fieldcorn and summer garden stuff for weeks save for the few frogs he'd shot. He knelt in the high grass and spoke to the fish where they stood in the clear water on wimpling fins. Ain't you a fine fat son of a bitch, he said.

He fairly loped toward the house. When he came back he had the rifle. He made his way along the creek and eased himself through the sedge and briers. He checked the sun to see it would not be in his eyes, making his way on all fours, the rifle cocked. He peered over the bank. Then he raised up on his knees. Then he stood up. Upstream below the ford Waldrop's cattle stood belly deep in the creek.

You sons of bitches, croaked Ballard. The creek was thick red with mud. He brought the rifle up and leveled it and fired. The cattle veered and surged in the red water, their eyes white. One of them made its way toward the bank holding its head at an odd angle. At the bank it slipped and fell and rose again. Ballard watched it with his jaw knotted. Oh shit, he said.

I'LL TELL YE another thing he done one time. He had this old cow to balk on him, couldn't get her to do nothin. He pushed and pulled and beat on her till she'd wore him out. He went and borry'd Squire Helton's tractor and went back over there and thowed a rope over the old cow's head and took off on the tractor hard as he could go. When it took up the slack it like to of jerked her head plumb off. Broke her neck and killed her where she stood. Ast Floyd if he didn't.

I don't know what he had on Waldrop that Waldrop never would run him off. Even after he burnt his old place down he never said nothin to him about it that I know of.

That reminds me of that Trantham boy had them old-timey oxes over at the fair here a year or two back. They sulled up on him and wouldn't go till finally he took and built a fire in underneath of em. The old oxes looked down and seen it and took about five steps and quit again. Trantham boy looked and there set the fire directly in under his wagon. He hollered and crawled up under the wagon and commenced a beatin at the fire with his hat and about that time them old oxes took off again. Drug the wagon over him and like to broke both his legs. You never seen more contrary beasts than them was.

COME UP, Lester, said the dumpkeeper.

Ballard was coming, he didn't need asking. Howdy Reubel, he said.

They sat in the sofa and looked at the ground, the old man tapping his stick up and down, Ballard holding the rifle upright between his knees.

When we goin to shoot some more rats? said the old man.

Ballard spat. Any time you want, he said.

They about to carry us off out here.

Ballard cut his eyes toward the house where he'd seen a half naked girl cross in the gloom. A baby was crying.

I don't reckon you've seen em have ye?

What's that?

Hernie and that next to least'n.

Where they at?

I don't know, said the old man. They cut out, I reckon. Been gone three days.

That fairheaded one?

Yeah. Her and Hernie. I reckon they've took off with some of these here jellybeans.

Well, said Ballard.

I don't know what makes them girls so wild. Their grandmother was the biggest woman for churchgoin you ever seen. Where you goin, Lester?

I got to go.

Best not rush off in the heat of the day.

Yeah, said Ballard. I'm goin to walk out thisaway.

You see any rats, why, just shoot em.

If I see any.

You'll see some.

A dog followed him out the quarry road. Ballard gave a little dry whistle and snapped his fingers and the dog sniffed at his cuff. They went on up the road.

Ballard descended by giant stone stairs to the dry floor of the quarry. The great rock walls with their cannelured faces and featherdrill holes composed about him an enormous amphitheatre. The ruins of an old truck lay rusting in the honeysuckle. He crossed the corrugated stone floor among chips and spalls of stone. The truck looked like it had been machine-gunned. At the far end of the quarry was a rubble tip and Ballard stopped to search for artifacts, tilting old stoves and water heaters, inspecting bicycle parts and corroded buckets. He salvaged a worn kitchen knife with a chewed handle. He called the dog, his voice relaying from rock to rock and back again.

When he came out to the road again a wind had come up. A door somewhere was banging, an eerie sound in the empty wood. Ballard walked up the road. He passed a rusted tin shed and beyond it a wooden tower. He looked up. High up on the tower a door creaked open and clapped shut. Ballard looked around. Sheets of roofing tin clattered and banged and a white dust was blowing off the barren yard by the quarry shed. Ballard squinted in the dust going up the road. By the time he got to the county road it had begun to spit rain. He called the dog once more and he waited and then he went on.

THE WEATHER turned overnight. With the fall the sky grew bluer than he'd ever known. Or could remember. He sat hourlong in the windy sedge with the sun on his back. As if he'd store the warmth of it against the coming winter. He watched a cornpicker go snarling through the fields and in the evening he and the doves went husbanding among the chewed and broken stalks and he gathered several sackfuls and carried them to the cabin before dark.

The hardwood trees on the mountain subsided into yellow and flame and to ultimate nakedness. An early winter fell, a cold wind sucked among the black and barren branches. Alone in the empty shell of a house the squatter watched through the moteblown glass a rimshard of bone-colored moon come cradling up over the black balsams on the ridge, ink trees a facile hand had sketched against the paler dark of winter heavens.

A man much for himself. Drinkers gone to Kirby's would see him on the road by night, slouched and solitary, the rifle hanging in his hand as if it were a thing he could not get shut of.

He'd grown lean and bitter.

Some said mad.

A malign star kept him.

He stood in the crossroads listening to other men's hounds on the mountain. A figure of wretched arrogance in the lights of the few cars passing. In their coiling dust he cursed or muttered or spat after them, the men tightly shouldered in the high old sedans with guns and jars of whiskey among them and lean treedogs curled in the turtle-deck.

One cold morning on the Frog Mountain turnaround he found a lady sleeping under the trees in a white gown. He watched her for a while to see if she were dead. He threw a rock or two, one touched her leg. She stirred heavily, her hair all caught with leaves. He went closer. He could see her heavy breasts sprawled under the thin stuff of her nightdress and he could see the dark thatch of hair under her belly. He knelt and touched her. Her slack mouth twisted. Her eyes opened. They seemed to open downward by the underlids like a bird's and her eyeballs were gorged with blood. She sat up suddenly, a sweet ferment of whiskey and rot coming off her. Her lip drew back in a cat's snarl. What do you want, you son of a bitch? she said.

Ain't you cold?

What the hell is it to you?

It ain't a damn thing to me.

Ballard had risen and stood above her with the rifle.

Where's your clothes at?

She rose up and staggered backwards and sat down hard in the leaves. Then she got up again. She stood there weaving and glaring at him with her puffed and heavylidded eyes. Son of a bitch, she said. Her eyes were casting about. Spying a rock, she lunged and scrabbled it up and stood him off with it.

Ballard's eyes narrowed. You better put down that rock, he said.

You make me.

I said to put it down.

She drew the rock back menacingly. He took a step forward. She heaved the rock and hit him in the chest with it and then covered her face with her hands. He slapped her so hard it spun her back around facing him. She said: I knowed you'd do me thisaway.

Ballard touched his hand to his chest and glanced down quickly to check for blood but there was none. She had her face buried in her hands. He took hold of the strap of her gown and gave it a good yank. The thin material parted to the waist. She turned loose of her face and grabbed at the gown. Her nipples were hard and bluelooking with the cold. Quit, she said.

Ballard seized a fistful of the wispy rayon and snatched it. Her feet came from under her and she sat in the trampled frozen weeds. He folded the garment under his arm and stepped back. Then he turned and went on down the road. She sat stark naked on the ground and watched him go, calling various names after him, none his.

FATE'S ALL RIGHT. He's plainspoken but I like him. I've rode with him a lot of times. I remember one night up on the Frog Mountain at the turnaround there they was a car parked up there and Fate put the lights on em and walked on up there. The old boy in the car was all yessir and nosir. Had this girl with him. He ast the old boy for his license and the old boy scratched around for the longest time, couldn't find his pocketbook nor nothin. Fate finally told him, said: Step out here. Said the old girl settin there was white as a sheet. Well, the old boy opened the door and out he steps. Fate looked at him and then he hollered at me, said: John, come here and see this.

I went on up there and the old boy is standin by the side of the car lookin down and the sheriff is lookin down, got the light on him. We're all standin there lookin down at this old boy and he's got his britches on inside out. Pockets hangin outside all around. Looked crazier'n hell. Sheriff just told him to go on. Ast him if he could drive like that. That's the kind of feller he is.

WHEN BALLARD came out onto the porch there was a thin man with a collapsed jaw squatting in the yard waiting for him.

What say Darfuzzle, said Ballard.

What say Lester.

He sounded like a man with a mouthful of marbles, articulating his goatbone underjaw laboriously, the original one having been shot away.

Ballard squatted on his heels in the yard opposite the visitor. They looked like constipated gargoyles.

Say you found that old gal up on the turnaround?

Ballard sniffed. What gal? he said.

Thatn was left up yonder. Had on a nightgown.

Ballard pulled at the loose sole of his shoe. I seen her, he said.

She's went to the sheriff.

She has?

The other man turned and spat and looked back toward Ballard. They done arrested Pless.

That's your all's lookout. I didn't have nothin to do with her.

She says you did.

She's a lyin sack of green shit.

The visitor rose. I just thought I'd tell ye, he said. You do what you want.

THE HIGH SHERIFF of Sevier County came out through the courthouse doors and stood on the portico surveying the gray lawn below with the benches and the Sevier County pocketknife society that convened there to whittle and mutter and spit. He rolled a cigarette and replaced the package of tobacco in the breast pocket of his tailored shirt and lit the cigarette and descended the stairs, a proprietary squint to his eyes as he studied the morning aspect of this small upland county seat.

A man opened the door and called down to him and the sheriff turned.

Mr Gibson's huntin you, the man said.

You don't know where I'm at.

Okay.

And where the hell is Cotton?

He's went to get the car.

He better get his ass on up here.

Yonder he comes now, Sheriff.

The sheriff turned and went on out to the street.

Mornin Sheriff.

Mornin.

Mornin Sheriff.

Hey. How you.

He flipped the cigarette into the street and stepped into the car and pulled the door to. Mornin Sheriff, said the driver.

Let's go get the little fucker, said the sheriff.

Me and Bill Parsons was goin to go birdhuntin this mornin but I don't reckon we will now.

Bill Parsons eh?

He's got a couple of good dogs.

O yeah. He always has the best dogs. I remember a dog he had one time named Suzie he said was a hellatious bird dog. He let her out of the trunk and I looked at her and I said: I don't believe Suzie's feelin too good. He looked at her and felt her nose and all. Said she looked all right to him. I told him, said: I just don't believe she's real well today. We set out and hunted all afternoon and killed one bird. Started walkin back to the car and he says to me, Bill says: You know, it's funny you noticin old Suzie was not feelin good today. The way you spotted it. I said: Well, Suzie was sick today. He said yes, she was. I said: Suzie was sick yesterday. Suzie has always been sick. Suzie will always be sick. Suzie is a sick dog.

HE WATCHED the sheriff stop out on the road a quarter mile away and he watched him ford the sheer wall of dried briers and weeds at the edge of the road and come on with arms and elbows aloft, treading down the brush. When he got to the house his pressed and tailored chinos were dusty and wilted and he was covered with dead beggarlice and burrs and he was not happy.

Ballard stood on the porch.

Let's go, said the sheriff.

Where to?

You better get your ass down off that porch.

Ballard spat and unleaned himself from the porchpost. You got it all, he said. He came down the steps, his hands in the rear pockets of his jeans.

Man of leisure like yourself, the sheriff said. You oughtn't to mind helpin us workers unscramble a little misunderstandin. This way, mister.

This way, said Ballard. They's a path if you don't know it.


BALLARD IN A varnished oak swivelchair. He leans back. The door is pebblegrain glass. Shadows loom upon it. The door opens. A deputy comes in and turns around. There is a woman behind him. When she sees Ballard she starts to laugh. Ballard is craning his neck to see her. She comes through the door and stands looking at him. He looks down at his knee. He begins to scratch his knee.

The sheriff got up from his desk. Shut the door, Cotton.

This son of a bitch here, the woman said, pointing at Ballard. Where the hell did you find him at?

Is he not the one?

Well. Yes. He's the one, the one . . . It's them other two sons of bitches I want jailed. This son of a bitch here . . . She threw up her hands in disgust.

Ballard scuffed one heel along the floor. I ain't done nothin, he said.

Did you want to make a charge against this man or not?

Hell yes I do.

What did you want to charge him with?

Rape, by god.

Ballard laughed woodenly.

Salt and battery too, you son of a bitch.

She ain't nothin but a goddamned old whore.

The old whore slapped Ballard's mouth. Ballard came up

from the swivelchair and began to choke her. She brought her knee up into his groin. They grappled. They fell backward upsetting a tin wastebasket. A halltree toppled with its load of coats. The sheriff's deputy seized Ballard by the collar. Ballard wheeled. The woman was screaming. The three of them crashed to the floor.

The deputy jerked Ballard's arm up behind him. He was livid.

You goddamned bitch, Ballard said.

Get her, the sheriff said. Get . . .

The deputy had one knee in the small of Ballard's back. The woman had risen. She cocked her elbows and drew back her foot and kicked Ballard in the side of the head.

Here now, said the deputy. She kicked again. He grabbed her foot and she sat down in the floor. Goddamn it Sheriff, he said, get her or him one, will ye?

You sons of bitches, said Ballard. He was almost crying. Goddamn all of ye.

Bet me, said the woman. I'll kick his goddamned cods off. The son of a bitch.


NINE DAYS and nights in the Sevier County jail. Whitebeans with fatback and boiled greens and baloney sandwiches on lightbread. Ballard thought the fare not bad. He even liked the coffee.

They had a nigger in the cell opposite and the nigger used to sing all the time. He was being held on a fugitive warrant. After a day or two Ballard fell into talking with him. He said: What's your name?

John, said the nigger. Nigger John.

Where you from. You a fugitive ain't ye?

I'm from Pine Bluff Arkansas and I'm a fugitive from the ways of this world. I'd be a fugitive from my mind if I had me some snow.

What you in for?

I cut a motherfucker's head off with a pocketknife.

Ballard waited to be asked his own crime but he wasn't asked. After a while he said: I was supposed to of raped this old girl. She wasn't nothin but a whore to start with.

White pussy is nothin but trouble.

Ballard agreed that it was. He guessed he'd thought so but he'd never heard it put that way.

The black sat on his cot and rocked back and forth. He crooned:

> Flyin home
> Fly like a motherfucker
> Flyin home

All the trouble I ever was in, said Ballard, was caused by whiskey or women or both. He'd often heard men say as much.

All the trouble I ever was in was caused by gettin caught, said the black.

After a week the sheriff came down the corridor one day and took the nigger away. Flyin home, sang the nigger.

You'll be flyin all right, said the sheriff. Home to your maker.

Fly like a motherfucker, sang the nigger.

Take it easy, called Ballard.

The nigger didn't say if he would or wouldn't.

The next day the sheriff came again and stopped in front of Ballard's cage and peered in at him. Ballard peered back. The sheriff had a straw in his teeth and he took it out to speak. He said: Where was that woman from?

What woman?

That one you raped.

You mean that old whore?

All right. That old whore.

I don't know. How the hell would I know where she was from?

Was she from Sevier County?

I don't know, damn it.

The sheriff looked at him and put the straw back in his teeth and went away.

They came for Ballard the next morning, turnkey and bailiff.

Ballard, the turnkey said.

Yeah.

He followed the bailiff down the corridor. The turnkey followed. They went downstairs, Ballard easing himself along the iron banister pipe. They went outside and across a parking lot to the courthouse.

They sat him in a chair in an empty room. He could see

a thin strip of color and movement through the gap of the double doors and he listened vaguely to legal proceedings. After an hour or so the bailiff came in and crooked his finger at Ballard. Ballard rose and went through the doors and sat in a church-bench behind a little rail.

He heard his name. He closed his eyes. He opened them again. A man in a white shirt at the desk looked at him and looked at some papers and then he looked at the sheriff. Since when? he said.

It's been a week or better.

Well tell him to get on out of here.

The bailiff came over and opened the gate and leaned toward Ballard. You can go, he said.

Ballard stood up and went through the gate and across the room toward a door with daylight in it and across a hall and out through the front door of the Sevier County courthouse. No one called him back. A drooling man at the door held out a greasy hat at him and mumbled something. Ballard went down the steps and crossed the street.

Uptown he walked around in the stores. He went into the postoffice and looked through the sheaves of posters. The wanted stared back with surly eyes. Men of many names. Their tattoos. Legends of dead loves inscribed on perishable flesh. A prevalence of blue panthers.

He was standing in the street with his hands in his back pockets when the sheriff walked up.

What's your plans now? said the sheriff.

Go home, said Ballard.

And what then. What sort of meanness have you got laid out for next.

I ain't got any laid out.

I figure you ought to give us a clue. Make it more fair. Let's see: failure to comply with a court order, public disturbance, assault and battery, public drunk, rape. I guess murder is next on the list ain't it? Or what things is it you've done that we ain't found out yet.

I ain't done nothin, Ballard said. You just got it in for me.

The sheriff had his arms folded and he was rocking slightly on his heels, studying the sullen reprobate before him. Well, he said. I guess you better get your ass on home. These people here in town won't put up with your shit.

I ain't ast nothin from nobody in this chickenshit town.

You better get your ass on home, Ballard.

Ain't a goddamn thing keepin me here cept you goin on at the mouth.

The sheriff stepped from in front of him. Ballard went on by and up the street. About halfway along the block he looked back. The sheriff was still watching him.

You kindly got henhouse ways yourself, Sheriff, he said.

HE HAD THAT RIFLE from when he was just almost a boy. He worked for old man Whaley settin fenceposts at eight cents a post to buy it. Told me he quit midmornin right in the middle of the field the day he got enough money. I don't remember what he give for it but I think it come to over seven hundred posts.

I'll say one thing. He could by god shoot it. Hit anything he could see. I seen him shoot a spider out of a web in the top of a big redoak one time and we was far from the tree as from here to the road yonder.

They run him off out at the fair one time. Wouldn't let him shoot no more.

I remember back a number of years, talkin about fairs, they had a old boy come through would shoot live pigeons with ye. Him with a rifle and you with a shotgun. Or anything else. He must of had a truckload of pigeons. Had a boy out in the middle of a field with a crateful and he'd holler and the boy'd let one slip and he'd raise his rifle and blam, he'd

55

dust it. Misters, he could strictly make the feathers fly. We'd never seen the like of shootin. They was a bunch of us pretty hotshot birdhunters lost our money out there fore we got it figured out. What he was doin, this boy was loadin the old pigeons up the ass with them little firecrackers. They'd take off like they was home free and get up about so high and blam, it'd blow their asses out. He'd just shoot directly he seen the feathers fly. You couldn't tell it. Or I take that back, somebody did finally. I don't remember who it was. Reached and grabbed the rifle out of the old boy's hand fore he could shoot and the old pigeon just went blam anyways. They like to tarred and feathered him over it.

That reminds me of this carnival they had up in Newport one time. They was a feller up there had this ape or gorilla, ever what it was, stood about so high. It was nigh tall as Jimmy yonder. They had it to where you could put on boxin gloves and get in this ring with it and if you could stay in there with him three minutes they'd give ye fifty dollars.

Well, these old boys I was with they kept at me and kept at me. I had this little old gal on my arm kept look in up at me about like a poleaxed calf. These old boys eggin me on. I think we'd drunk a little whiskey too, I disremember. Anyways I got to studyin this here ape and I thought: Well hell. He ain't big as me. They had him up there on a chain. I remember he was settin on a stool eatin a head of red cabbage. Directly I said: Shit. Raised my old hand and told the feller I'd try it one time.

Well, they got us back there and got the gloves on me

and all, and this feller that owned the ape, he told me, said: Now don't hit him too hard out there cause if you do you'll make him mad and you'll be in some real trouble. I thought to myself: Well he's tryin to save his ape a whippin is what he's tryin to do. Tryin to protect his investment.

Anyways, I come out and climbed in the ring there. Felt pretty much a fool, all my buddies out there a hollerin and goin on and I looked down at this little gal I was with and give her a big wink and about that time they brought the old ape out. Had a muzzle on him. He kindly looked me over. Well, they called out our names and everthing, I forget what the old ape's name was, and this old boy rung a big dinner bell and I stepped out and circled the old ape. Showed him a little footwork there. He didn't look like he was goin to do nothin much so I reached out and busted him one. He just kindly looked at me. Well, I didn't do nothin but square off and hit him again. Popped him right in the side of the head. When I done that his old head jerked back and his eyes went kindly funny and I said: Well, well, how sweet it is. I'd done spent the fifty dollars. I ducked around and went to hit him again and about that time he jumped right on top of my head and crammed his foot in my mouth and like to tore my jaw off. I couldn't even holler for help. I thought they never would get that thing off of me.

BALLARD AMONG the fairgoers stepping gingerly through the mud. Down sawdust lanes among the pitchtents and lights and cones of cottoncandy and past painted stalls with tiers of prizes and dolls and animals dangling from guyropes. A ferriswheel stood against the sky like a gaudy bracelet and little hawkwinged goatsuckers shuttled among the upflung strobes of light with gape mouths and weird cries.

Where celluloid goldfish bobbed in a tank he leaned with his dipnet and watched the other fishers. An attendant took the fish from their nets and read the numbers on their undersides and shook his head no or reached down a small kewpie or a plaster cat. While he was so occupied an old man next to Ballard was trying to steer two fish into his dipnet at the same time. They would not fit and the old man grown impatient steered them to the edge of the tank and with a sweep of the net splashed fish and water down the front of a woman standing next to him. The woman looked down. The fish were lying in the grass. You must be crazy, she said. Or drunk one. The old man gripped his net. The attendant leaned to them. What's the matter here, he said.

I didn't do nothin, said the old man.

Ballard was dipping up fish and dumping them back, studying the numbers on the prizes. The woman with the wet dress pointed at him. That man yonder is cheatin, she said.

Okay buddy, said the attendant, reaching for his net. You get one for a dime, three for a quarter.

I ain't got one yet, said Ballard.

You've done put back a dozen.

I ain't got one, said Ballard, holding his net.

Well get one and look at the rest.

Ballard shrugged up his shoulders and eyed the fish. He dipped one up.

The attendant took the fish and looked at it. No winner, he said, and pitched the fish back in the tank and took the net from Ballard.

I might not be done playin, said Ballard.

And then again you might, said the attendant.

Ballard gave the man a cold cat's look and spat in the water and turned to go. The lady who'd been splashed was watching him with a half fearful look of vindication. As Ballard went past he spoke to her through his teeth. You a busynosed old whore, ain't ye? he said.

He stirred as he went the weight of dimes in the toe of his pocket. Riflefire guided him, a muted sound that he sorted from among the cries of barkers and pitchmen. A busy booth with longlegged boys crouched at the counter. Across the back of the gallery mechanical ducks tottered and creaked and the rifles cracked and spat.

Step right up, step right up, test your skill and win a prize, sang the shooting gallery man. Yes sir, how about you?

I'm studyin it, said Ballard. What do ye get?

The pitchman pointed with his cane to rows of stuffed animals in ascending size. The bottom row, he said . . .

Never mind them, said Ballard. What do you have to do to get them big'ns yonder.

The pitchman pointed to small cards on a wire. Shoot out the small red dot, he said in a singsong voice. You have five shots in which to do it and you take your choice of any prize in the house.

Ballard had his dimes out. How much is it? he said.

Twenty-five cents.

He laid three dimes on the counter. The pitchman stood a rifle up and slid a brass tube of shells into the magazine. It was a pump rifle and it was fastened to the counter by a chain.

Ballard put the nickel in his pocket and raised the rifle.

Elbow rests permitted, sang the pitchman.

I don't need no rest, said Ballard. He fired five times, lowering the rifle between rounds. When he was done he pointed aloft. Let me have that there big bear, he said.

The pitchman trolleyed the little card down a wire and unpinned it and handed it to Ballard. All of the red must be removed from the card to win, he said. He was looking elsewhere and didn't even seem to be talking to Ballard.

Ballard took the card in his hand and looked at it. You mean this here? he said.

All of the red must be removed.

Ballard's card had a single hole in the middle of it. Along one edge of the hole was the faintest piece of red lint.

Why hell fire, said Ballard. He slapped three more dimes on the counter. Step right up, said the pitchman, loading the rifle.

When the card came back you could'nt have found any red on it with a microscope. The pitchman handed down a ponderous mohair teddybear and Ballard slapped down three dimes again.

When he had won two bears and a tiger and a small audience the pitchman took the rifle away from him. That's it for you, buddy, he hissed.

You never said nothin about how many times you could win.

Step right up, sang the barker. Who's next now. Three big grand prizes per person is the house limit. Who's our next big winner.

Ballard loaded up his bears and the tiger and started off through the crowd. They lord look at what all he's won, said a woman. Ballard smiled tightly. Young girls' faces floated past, bland and smooth as cream. Some eyed his toys. The crowd was moving toward the edge of a field and assembling there, Ballard among them, a sea of country people watching into the dark for some midnight contest to begin.

A light sputtered off in the field and a bluetailed rocket went skittering toward Canis Major. High above their upturned faces it burst, sprays of lit glycerine flaring across the night, trailing down the sky in loosely falling ribbons of hot spectra soon burnt to naught. Another went up, a long whishing sound, fishtailing aloft. In the bloom of its opening you could see like its shadow the image of the rocket gone before, the puff of black smoke and ashen trails arcing out and down like a huge and dark medusa squatting in the sky. In the bloom of light too you could see two men out in the field crouched over their crate of fireworks like assassins or bridgeblowers. And you could see among the faces a young girl with candyapple on her lips and her eyes wide. Her pale hair smelled of soap, womanchild from beyond the years, rapt below the sulphur glow and pitchlight of some medieval fun fair. A lean skylong candle skewered the black pools in her eyes. Her fingers clutched. In the flood of this breaking brimstone galaxy she saw the man with the bears watching her and she edged closer to the girl by her side and brushed her hair with two fingers quickly.

BALLARD HAS come in from the dark dragging sheaves of snowclogged bracken and he has fallen to crushing up handfuls of this dried or frozen stuff and cramming it into the fireplace. The lamp in the floor gutters in the wind and wind moans in the flue. The cracks in the wall lie printed slantwise over the floorboards in threads of drifted snow and wind is shucking the cardboard windowpanes. And Ballard has come with an armload of beanpoles purloined from the barnloft and he is at breaking them and laying them on.

When he has the fire going he pulls off his brogans and stands them on the hearth and he pulls the wadded socks from his toes and lays them out to dry. He sits and dries the rifle and ejects the shells into his lap and dries them and wipes the action and oils it and oils the receiver and the barrel and the magazine and the lever and reloads the rifle and levers a shell into the chamber and lets the hammer down and lays the rifle on the floor beside him.

The cornbread he has baked in the fire is a crude mush

of simple meal and water. A flat tasteless crust that he chews woodenly and washes down with water. The two bears and the tiger watch from the wall, their plastic eyes shining in the firelight and their red flannel tongues out.

THE HOUNDS CROSSED the snow on the slope of the ridge in a thin dark line. Far below them the boar they trailed was tilting along with his curious stifflegged lope, highbacked and very black against the winter's landscape. The hounds' voices in that vast and pale blue void echoed like the cries of demon yodelers.

The boar did not want to cross the river. When he did so it was too late. He came all sleek and steaming out of the willows on the near side and started across the plain. Behind him the dogs were falling down the mountainside hysterically, the snow exploding about them. When they struck the water they smoked like hot stones and when they came out of the brush and onto the plain they came in clouds of pale vapor.

The boar did not turn until the first hound reached him. He spun and cut at the dog and went on. The dogs swarmed over his hindquarters and he turned and hooked with his razorous tushes and reared back on his haunches but there was nothing for shelter. He kept turning, enmeshed in a wheel of snarling hounds until he caught one and drove upon it and pinned and disemboweled it. When he went to turn again to save his flanks he could not.

Ballard watched this ballet tilt and swirl and churn mud up through the snow and watched the lovely blood welter there in its holograph of battle, spray burst from a ruptured lung, the dark heart's blood, pinwheel and pirouette, until shots rang and all was done. A young hound worried the boar's ears and one lay dead with his bright ropy innards folded upon the snow and another whined and dragged himself about. Ballard took his hands from his pockets and took up the rifle from where he had leaned it against a tree. Two small armed and upright figures were moving down along the river, hurrying against the fading light.

In the smith's shop and near lightless save for the faint glow at the far end where the forge fire smoldered and the smith in silhouette hulked above some work. Ballard in the door with a rusty axehead he'd found.

Mornin, said the smith.

Mornin.

What can I do for ye?

I got a axe needs sharpenin.

He crossed the dirt floor to where the smith stood above his anvil. The walls of the building were hung with all manner of implements. Pieces of farm machinery and motorcars lay strewn everywhere.

The smith thrust his chin forward and looked at the axehead. That it? he said.

That's it.

The smith turned the axehead in his hand. Won't do ye no good to grind this thing, he said.

Won't?

What ye aim to use for a handle?

Get one, I reckon.

He held the axehead up. You cain't just grind a axe and grind it, he said. See how stobby it's got?

Ballard saw.

You want to wait a minute I'll show ye how to dress a axe that'll cut two to one against any piece of shit you can buy down here at the hardware store brand new.

What'll it cost me?

You mean with a new handle and all.

Yeah, with a new handle.

Cost ye two dollars.

Two dollars.

That's right. Handles is a dollar and a quarter.

I allowed I'd just get it sharpened for a quarter or somethin.

You never would be satisfied with it, said the smith.

I can get a new one for four dollars.

I'd better to have thisn and it right than two new ones.

Well.

Tell me somethin.

All right.

The smith stuck the axe in the fire and gave the crank a few turns. Yellow flames spat out from under the blade. They watched.

You want to keep your fire high, said the smith. Three or

four inches above the tuyer iron. You want to lay a clean fire with good coal that's not laid out in the sun.

He turned the axehead with his tongs. You want to take your first heat at a good yeller and work down. That there ain't hot enough. He had raised his voice to make these observations although the forge made no sound. He cranked the lever again and they watched the fire spit.

Not too fast, said the smith. Slow. That's how ye heat. Watch ye colors. If she chance to get white she's ruint. There she comes now.

He drew the axehead from the fire and swung it all quivering with heat and glowing a translucent yellow and laid it on the anvil.

Now mind how ye work only the flats, he said, taking up his hammer. And start on the bit. He swung the hammer and the soft steel gave under the blow with an odd dull ring. He hammered out the bit on both sides and put the blade back in the fire.

We take another heat on her only not so high this time. A high red color will do it. He laid the tongs on the anvil and passed both palms down hard over his apron, his eyes on the fire. Watch her well, he said. Never leave steel in the fire for longer than it takes to heat. Some people will poke around at somethin else and leave the tool they're heatin to perdition but the proper thing is to fetch her out the minute she shows the color of grace. Now we want a high red. Want a high red. Now she comes.

He tonged the axehead to the anvil again, the bit a deep orange color with pins of bright heat breaking on it.

See now do ye hammer her back from the bit on the second heat.

The hammer striking with that sound not quite metallic.

About a inch back. See how she flares. Let her get wide as a shovel if it takes it but never lay your hammer to the edges or you'll take out the muscle you put in on the flats.

He hammered steady and effortless, the bit cooling until the light of it faded to a faintly pulsing blood color. Ballard glanced about the shop. The smith laid the bit on the hardy and with a sledge clipped off the flared edges. That's how we take the width down, he said. Now one more heat to make her tough.

He placed the blade in the fire and cranked the handle. We take a low heat this time, he said. Just for a minute. Just so ye can see her shine will do. There she is.

Now hammer her down both sides real good. He beat with short strokes. He turned the head and worked the other side. See how black she gets, he said. Black and shiny like a nigger's ass. That packs the steel and makes it tough. Now she's ready to harden.

They waited while the axe heated. The smith took a splayed cigarstub from his apron pocket and lit it with a coal from the forge. We just want to heat the part we've worked, he said. And the lower a heat ye can harden at the better she'll be. Just a low cherry red is about right. Some people want to quench in oil but water tempers at a lower heat. A little salt to soften the water. Soft water, hard steel. Now she comes and mind how when ye take her up and dip, dip north. Bit straight down, thisaway. He lowered the quaking blade into the quenchbucket and a ball of steam rose. The metal hissed for an instant and was quiet. The smith dunked it up and down. Cool it slow and it won't crack, he said. Now. We polish it and draw the temper.

He brightened the bit with a stick wrapped in emery cloth. Holding the head in the tongs he began to move it slowly back and forth over the fire. Keep her out of the fire and keep her movin. That way she'll draw down even. Now she's gettin yeller. That's fine for some tools but we goin to take a blue temper on her. Now she gets brown. Watch it now. See it there?

He took the axehead from the fire and laid it on the anvil. You got to watch her close and not let the temper run out on the corners first. Shape ye fire for the job always.

Is that it? said Ballard.

That's it. We'll just fit ye a handle now and sharpen her and you'll be on your way.

Ballard nodded.

It's like a lot of things, said the smith. Do the least part of it wrong and ye'd just as well to do it all wrong. He was sorting through handles standing in a barrel. Reckon you could do it now from watchin? he said.

Do what, said Ballard.

HE LAUNCHED HIMSELF down the slope, slewed up in snow to his thighs, wallowing in the drifts with the rifle held overhead in one hand. He caught himself on a grapevine and swung about and came to a stop. A shower of dead leaves and twigs fell over the smooth mantle of snow. He fetched debris from out of his shirtcollar and looked down the slope to find another stopping place.

When he reached the flats at the foot of the mountain he found himself in scrub cedar and pines. He followed rabbit paths through these woods. The snow had thawed and frozen over again and there was a light crust on top now and the day was very cold. He entered a glade and a robin flew. Another. They held their wings aloft and went skittering over the snow. Ballard looked more closely. A group of them were huddled under a cedar tree. At his approach they set forth in pairs and threes and went hopping and hobbling over the crust, dragging their wings. Ballard ran after them. They ducked and fluttered. He fell and rose and ran laughing. He caught and held one warm and feathered in his palm with the heart of it beating there just so.

HE CAME UP a rutted drive and past the roof of a car sliced off and propped on the ground with cinderblocks. A light-cord ran across the mud and underneath the car roof a bulb burned and a group of depressed looking chickens huddled and clucked. Ballard rapped on the porch floor. It was a cold gray day. Thick gouts of brownish smoke swirled over the roof and the rags of snow in the yard lay gray and lacy and flecked with coalsoot. He peeped down at the bird against his breast. The door opened.

Get in here, said a woman in a thin cotton housedress.

He went on up the porchsteps and entered the house. He spoke with the woman but his eye was on the daughter. She moved ill at ease about the house, all tits and plump young haunch and naked legs. Cold enough for ye? said Ballard.

What about this weather, said the woman.

I brung him a playpretty, Ballard said, nodding to the thing in the floor.

The woman turned her shallow dish-shaped face upon him. Done what? she said.

Brung him a playpretty. Looky here.

He hauled forth the half froze robin from his shirt and held it out. It turned its head. Its eye flicked.

Looky here, Billy, said the woman.

It didn't look. A hugeheaded bald and slobbering primate that inhabited the lower reaches of the house, familiar of the warped floorboards and the holes tacked up with foodtins hammered flat, a consort of roaches and great hairy spiders in their season, perennially benastied and afflicted with a nameless crud.

Here's ye a playpretty.

The robin started across the floor, its wings awobble like lateen sails. It spied the . . . what? child? child, and veered off toward a corner. The child's dull eyes followed. It stirred into sluggish motion.

Ballard caught the bird and handed it down. The child took it in fat gray hands.

He'll kill it, the girl said.

Ballard grinned at her. It's hisn to kill if he wants to, he said.

The girl pouted her mouth at him. Shoot, she said.

I got somethin I'm a goin to bring you, Ballard told her.

You ain't got nothin I want, she said.

Ballard grinned.

I got some coffee hot on the stove, said the woman from the kitchen. Did you want a cup?

I wouldn't care to drink maybe just a cup, said Ballard, rubbing his hands together to say how cold it was.

At the kitchen table, a huge white porcelain cup before him, the steam white in the cold of the room by the one window where he sat and the moisture condensing on the flower faded oilcloth. He tilted canned milk in and stirred.

What time do you reckon Ralph will be in?

He ain't said.

Well.

Just wait on him if ye want.

Well. I'll wait on him a minute. If he don't come I got to get on.

He heard the back door shut. He saw her go along the muddied rut of a path to the outhouse. He looked at the woman. She was rolling out biscuits at the sideboard. He looked quickly back out the window. The girl opened the outhouse door and closed it behind her. Ballard lowered his face into the steam from his cup.

Ralph didn't come and didn't come. Ballard finished the coffee and said that it was good and no thanks he didn't want no more and said it again and said that he'd better get on.

I wish you'd looky here Mama, the girl said from the other room.

What is it? said the woman.

Ballard had stood up and was stretching uneasily. I better get on, he said.

Just wait on him if ye want.

Mama.

Ballard looked toward the front room. The bird crouched in the floor. The girl appeared in the doorway. I wisht you'd look in here, she said.

What is it? said the woman.

She was pointing toward the child. It sat as before, a gross tottertoy in a gray small shirt. Its mouth was stained

75

with blood and it was chewing. Ballard went on through the door into the room and reached down to get the bird. It fluttered on the floor and fell over. He picked it up. Small red nubs worked in the soft down. Ballard set the bird down quickly.

I told ye not to let him have it, the girl said.

The bird floundered on the floor.

The woman had come to the door. She was wiping her hands on her apron. They were all looking at the bird. The woman said: What's he done to it?

He's done chewed its legs off, the girl said.

Ballard grinned uneasily. He wanted it to where it couldn't run off, he said.

If I didn't have no better sense than that I'd quit, said the girl.

Hush now, said the woman. Get that mess out of his mouth fore he gets sick on it.

THEY WASN'T none of em any account that I ever heard of. I remember his grandaddy, name was Leland, he was gettin a war pension as a old man. Died back in the late twenties. Was supposed to of been in the Union Army. It was a known fact he didn't do nothin the whole war but scout the bushes. They come lookin for him two or three times. Hell, he never did go to war. Old man Cameron tells this and I don't know what cause he'd have to lie. Said they come out there to get Leland Ballard and while they was huntin him in the barn and smokehouse and all he slipped down out of the bushes to where their horses was at and cut the leather off the sergeant's saddle to halfsole his shoes with.

No, I don't know how he got that pension. Lied to em, I reckon. Sevier County put more men in the Union Army than it had registered voters but he wasn't one of em. He was just the only one had brass enough to ast for a pension.

I'll tell you one thing he was if he wasn't no soldier. He was a by god White Cap.

O yes. He was that. Had a younger brother was one too that run off from here about that time. It's a known fact he was hanged in Hattiesburg Mississippi. Goes to show it ain't just the place. He'd of been hanged no matter where he lived.

I'll say one thing about Lester though. You can trace em back to Adam if you want and goddamn if he didn't outstrip em all.

That's the god's truth.

Talkin about Lester . . .

You all talk about him. I got supper waitin on me at the house.

# II

On a cold winter morning in the early part of December Ballard came down off Frog Mountain with a brace of squirrels hanging from his belt and emerged onto the Frog Mountain road. When he looked back toward the turnaround he saw that there was a car there with the motor chugging gently and blue smoke coiling into the cold morning air. Ballard crossed the road and dropped down off through the weeds and climbed up through the woods until he came out above the turnaround. The car sat idling as before. He could not see anyone inside.

He made his way along by the roadside growth until he was within thirty feet of the car and there he stood watching. He could hear the steady loping of the engine and he could hear somewhere faintly in the quiet mountainside morning the sound of a guitar and singing. After a while it stopped and he could hear a voice.

It's a radio, he said.

There was no sign of anyone in the car. The windows

were fogged but it didn't look like there was anyone in there.

He came out of the bushes and walked on down past the automobile. He was just a squirrelhunter going on down the road if it was anybody's business. When he passed the side of the automobile he looked in. The front seat was empty but in the back were two people half naked sprawled together. A bare thigh. An arm upflung. A hairy pair of buttocks. Ballard had kept on walking. Then he stopped. A pair of eyes staring with lidless fixity.

He turned and came back. With eyes uneasy he peered down through the window. Out of the disarray of clothes and the contorted limbs another's eyes watched sightlessly from a bland white face. It was a young girl. Ballard tapped at the glass. The man on the radio said: We'd like to dedicate this next number especially for all the sick and the shut-in. On the mountain two crows put forth, thin raucous calls in the cold and lonely air.

Ballard opened the car door, his rifle at the ready. The man lay sprawled between the girl's thighs. Hey, said Ballard.

Gathering flowers for the master's bouquet.

Beautiful flowers that will never decay

Ballard sat on the edge of the seat by the steering wheel and reached and turned the radio off. The motor went chug chug chug. He looked down and found the key and turned the ignition off. It was very quiet there in the car, just the three of them. He knelt in the seat and leaned over the back and studied the other two. He reached down and pulled the man by the shoulder. The man's arm dropped off the seat onto the floor of the car and Ballard, rearing up at this unexpected movement, banged his head on the roof.

He didn't even swear. He knelt there staring at the two bodies. Them sons of bitches is deader'n hell, he said.

He could see one of the girl's breasts. Her blouse was open and her brassiere was pushed up around her neck. Ballard stared for a long time. Finally he reached across the dead man's back and touched the breast. It was soft and cool. He stroked the full brown nipple with the ball of his thumb.

He was still holding the rifle. He backed off the seat and stood in the road and looked and listened. There was not even a birdcall to hear. He took the squirrels from his belt and laid them on top of the car and stood the rifle against the fender and got in again. Leaning over the seat he took hold of the man and tried to pull him off the girl. The body sprawled heavily, the head lolled. Ballard got him pulled sideways but he was jammed against the back of the front seat. He could see the girl better now. He reached and stroked her other breast. He did this for a while and then he pushed her eyes shut with his thumb. She was young and very pretty. Ballard shut the front door of the car against the cold. He reached down and got hold of the man again. He seemed to be hung. He was wearing a shirt and his trousers were collapsed about the tops of his shoes. With a sort of dull loathing Ballard seized the cold and naked hipbone and pulled him over. He rolled off and slid down between the seats onto the floor where he lay staring up with one eye open and one half shut.

They godamighty, said Ballard. The dead man's penis, sheathed in a wet yellow condom, was pointing at him rigidly.

He backed out of the car and picked up the rifle and walked out to where he could see down the road. He came back and shut the car door and walked around the other side. It was very cold. After a while he got in the car again. The girl lay with her eyes closed and her breasts peeking from her open blouse and her pale thighs spread. Ballard climbed over the seat.

The dead man was watching him from the floor of the car. Ballard kicked his feet out of the way and picked the girl's panties up from the floor and sniffed at them and put them in his pocket. He looked out the rear window and he listened. Kneeling there between the girl's legs he undid his buckle and lowered his trousers.

A crazed gymnast laboring over a cold corpse. He poured into that waxen ear everything he'd ever thought of saying to a woman. Who could say she did not hear him? When he'd finished he raised up and looked out again. The windows were fogged. He took the hem of the girl's skirt with which to wipe himself. He was standing on the dead man's legs. The dead man's member was still erect. Ballard pulled up his trousers and climbed over the seat and opened the door and stepped out into the road. He tucked in his shirt and buckled his breeches up. Then he picked up his rifle and started down the road. He hadn't gone far before he stopped and came back. The first thing he saw was the squirrels on the roof. He put them inside his shirt and opened the door and reached in and turned the key and pushed the starter button. It cranked loudly in the silence and the motor came to life. He looked at the gas gauge. The needle showed a quarter tank. He glanced at the bodies in the back and shut the door and started back down the road.

He had gone about a quarter mile before he stopped again. He stood there in the middle of the road staring straight ahead. Well kiss my ass, he said. He started back up the road. Then he started to run.

When he got to the car it was still chugging over and Ballard was out of breath and sucking long scoops of cold air down his throat into his seared lungs. He jerked open the door and climbed in and reached over the back seat and tugged at the dead man's trousers until he got to the back pocket and reached in and got hold of his wallet. He lifted it out and opened it. Family pictures within the little yellowed glassine windows. He took out a thin sheaf of bills and counted them. Eighteen dollars. He folded the money and stuck it in his pocket and put the wallet back in the man's trousers and climbed back out of the car and shut the door. He took the money out of his pocket and counted it again. He started to pick up the rifle but he paused and then climbed back into the car again.

He looked along the floor in the back and he looked along the seat and he felt under the bodies. Then he looked in the front. Her purse was on the floor by the side of the seat there. He opened it and took out her changepurse and opened it and took out a small handful of silver and two wadded dollar bills. He rummaged through the purse and took the lipstick and rouge and put them in his pocket and snapped the purse closed and sat there with it in his lap for a minute. Then he saw the glovebox in the dashboard. He reached and pushed the button and it fell open. Inside were papers and a flashlight and a pint bottle of bonded whiskey. Ballard fetched out the bottle and held it up. It was two thirds full. He closed the glovebox and climbed from the car and put the bottle in his pocket and shut the car door. He looked in at the girl once again and then he started down the road. He'd not gone but a few steps before he stopped and came back. He opened the car door and reached in and turned on the radio. Tuesday night we'll be at the Bulls Gap School, said the radio. Ballard shut the door and went on down the road. After a while he stopped and took out the bottle and drank and then he went on again.

He was almost to the roadfork at the foot of the mountain before he fetched up the final time. He turned around and looked back up the road. He squatted in the road and set the butt of the rifle down and gripping the forestock in both hands he rested his chin on one wrist. He spat. He looked at the sky. After a while he stood up and started back up the road. A hawk was riding the wind above the mountainside, turning the sun whitely from panel and underwing. It came about, flared, rode up. Ballard was hurrying up the road. His stomach was empty and tight.

WHEN HE GOT HOME with the dead girl it was midmorning. He had carried her on his shoulder for a mile before he gave out altogether. The two of them lying in the leaves in the woods. Ballard breathing quietly in the cold air. He hid the rifle and the squirrels in a windrow of black leaves beneath a ledge of limestone and struggled up with the girl and started off again.

He came down through the woods by the back of the house and through the wild grass and dead weeds past the barn and shouldered her through the narrow doorway and went in and laid her on the mattress and covered her. Then he went out with the axe.

He came in with an armload of firewood and got a fire going in the hearth and sat before it and rested. Then he turned to the girl. He took off all her clothes and looked at her, inspecting her body carefully, as if he would see how she were made. He went outside and looked in through the window at her lying naked before the fire. When he came back in he unbuckled his trousers and stepped out of them and laid next to her. He pulled the blanket over them.

IN THE AFTERNOON he went back for the rifle and the squirrels. He put the squirrels in his shirt and checked the breech of the rifle to see it was loaded and went on up the mountain.

When he came out through the stark winter woods above the turnaround the car was still there. The motor had stopped running. He squatted on his heels and watched. It was very quiet. He could hear the radio faintly below him. After a while he stood and spat and took a last survey of the scene and went back down the mountain.

In the morning when the black saplings stood like knives in the mist on the mountainside two boys came across the lot and entered the house where Ballard lay huddled in his blanket on the floor by the dead fire. The dead girl lay in the other room away from the heat for keeping.

They stood in the door. Ballard reared up with eyes walled and howled them out backward and half falling into the yard.

What the hell do you want? he yelled.

They stood in the yard. One had a rifle and one a homemade bow. This here's Charles's cousin, said the one with the rifle. You cain't run him off. We's told we could hunt here.

Ballard looked at the cousin. Get on and hunt then, he said.

Come on, Aaron, said the one with the rifle.

Aaron gave Ballard a grudging look and they went on across the yard.

You better stay away from here, called Ballard from the porch. He was shivering there in the cold. That's what you all better do.

When they had gone from sight in the dry weeds one of them called back something but Ballard could not make it out. He stood in the door where they'd stood and he looked into the room to see could he repeat with his own eyes what they'd seen. Nothing was certain. She lay beneath rags. He went in and built the fire back and squatted before it cursing.

When he came in from the barn he was dragging a crude homemade ladder and he took it into the room where the girl lay and raised the end of it up through a small square hole in the ceiling and climbed up and poked his head into the attic. The shake roof lay in a crazy jigsaw against the winter sky and in the checkered gloom he could make out a few old boxes filled with dusty mason jars. He climbed up and cleared a place on the loose loft floorboards and dusted them off with some rags and went back down again.

She was too heavy for him. He paused halfway up the ladder with one hand on the top rung and the other around the dead girl's waist where she dangled in the ripped and rudely sutured nightgown and then he descended again. He tried holding her around the neck. He got no farther. He sat on the floor with her, his breath exploding whitely in the cold of the room. Then he went out to the barn again.

He came in with some old lengths of plowline and sat before the fire and pieced them. Then he went in and fitted the rope about the waist of the pale cadaver and ascended the ladder with the other end. She rose slumpshouldered from the floor with her hair all down and began to bump slowly up the ladder. Halfway up she paused, dangling. Then she began to rise again.

HE HAD MADE the squirrels into a kind of stew with turnips and he set what was left of it before the fire to warm. After he had eaten he took the rifle up into the attic and left it and he took the ladder out and stood it by the back of the house. Then he went out to the road and started toward town.

Few cars passed. Ballard walking in the gray roadside grass among the beercans and trash did not even look up. It had grown colder and he was almost blue when he reached Sevierville three hours later.

Ballard shopping. Before a dry goods store where in the window a crude wood manikin headless and mounted on a pole wore a blowsy red dress.

He made several passes through the notions and dry goods, his hands on the money in his pockets. A salesgirl who stood with her arms crossed hugging her shoulders leaned to him as he passed.

Can I hep ye? she said.

I ain't looked good yet, said Ballard.

He made another sortie among the counters of lingerie, his eyes slightly wild as if in terror of the flimsy pastel garments there. When he came past the salesgirl again he put his hands in his rear pockets and tossed his head casually toward the display window. How much is that there red dress out front, he said.

She looked toward the front of the store and put her hand to her mouth for remembering. It's five ninety-eight, she said. Then she shook her head up and down. Yes. Five ninety-eight.

I'll take it, said Ballard.

The salesgirl unleaned herself from the counter. She and Ballard were about the same height. She said: What size did you need?

Ballard looked at her. Size, he said.

Did you know her size?

He rubbed his jaw. He'd never seen the girl standing up. He looked at the salesgirl. I don't know what size she takes, he said.

Well how big is she?

I don't believe she's big as you.

Do you know how much she weighs?

She'll weigh a hunnerd pound or better.

The girl looked at him sort of funny. She must be just small, she said.

She ain't real big.

They're over here, said the girl, leading the way.

They went creaking across the oiled wooden floors to a dress rack assembled out of galvanized waterpipe and the salesgirl fanned the hangers back and pulled out the red dress and held it up. This here's a seven, she said. I'd say it would fit her unless she's just teeninecy.

Okay, said Ballard.

She can swap it if it don't fit.

Okay.

She folded the dress across her arm. Was there anything else? she said.

Yeah, said Ballard. She needs some other stuff too.

The girl waited.

She needs some things to go with it.

What all does she need? the girl said.

She needs some drawers, Ballard blurted out.

The girl coughed into her fist and turned and went back up the aisle, Ballard behind, his face afire.

They stood at the counter he'd been studying all along from out of his eyecorner and the girl tapped her fingers on the little glass rail, looking past him. He stood with his hands still crammed in his rear pockets and his elbows out.

They's all these here, said the girl, taking a pencil from behind her ear and running it over the counter rail.

You got any black ones?

She rummaged through the stacks and came up with a pair of black ones with pink bows.

I'll take em, said Ballard. And one of them there.

She looked to where he was pointing. A slip? she said.

Yeah.

She moved along the counter. Here's a pretty red one, she said. Would go pretty with this dress.

Red? said Ballard.

She held it up.

I'll take that, said Ballard.

What else now? she said.

I don't know, said Ballard, casting his eye over the counter.

Does she need a bra?

No. You ain't got them drawers in the red have ye?


WHEN BALLARD reached Fox's store he was half frozen. A bluish dusk suffused the barren woods about. He went straight to the stove and stood next to the dusty gray barrel of it with his teeth chattering.

Cold enough for ye? said Mr Fox.

Ballard nodded.

Radio says it's goin down to three degrees tonight.

Ballard was not for smalltalk. He went around the store selecting cans of beans and vienna sausages and he got two loaves of bread and pointed out the baloney in the meatcase that he wanted a halfpound of and he got a quart of sweetmilk and some cheese and crackers and a box of cakes. Mr Fox totted up the bill on a scratchpad, assessing the items on the counter from over the tops of his glasses as he went. Ballard had his parcels from town tucked tightly in his armpit.

What about that boy they found up here yesterday evenin? Mr Fox said.

What about him, said Ballard.

HE GOT A fire going in the hearth and with wooden fingers undid the frozen lacings of his shoes and levered them from the shank of his foot, banging the heels on the floor until they came off. He looked at his feet. They were a pale yellow with white spots. When he went into the other room he could hardly feel the floor. He seemed to be walking about on his anklebones. He went out barefooted and fetched in the ladder and climbed up and looked at the girl. He came back down with the rifle and stood it by the fireplace. Then he opened the parcels from town and held up the garments and sniffed at them and folded them away again.

He opened a can of beans and a can of the sausages and set them in the fire and he put a pan of water on to make coffee with. Then he put the other things away in the closet and sitting on the edge of the mattress pulled on his shoes again. With the axe in his hand he went clopping across the floor and out into the night. It had begun to snow again.

He hauled wood until the room was a huge brush pile

with old pieces of stumps and whole lengths of fencepost with sections of rotted wire hanging from their staples. He worked at it until well past dark and got a good fire going and sat before it and ate his supper. When he was done he lit the lamp and went into the other room with it and climbed the ladder. Muttered curses, sounds of struggle, ensued.

She came down the ladder until she touched the floor with her feet and there she stopped. He paid out more rope but she was standing there in the floor leaning against the ladder. She was standing on tiptoe, nor would she fold. Ballard came down the ladder and undid the rope from around her waist. Then he dragged her into the other room and laid her on the hearth. He took hold of her arm and tried to raise it but the whole body shifted woodenly. Goddamn frozen bitch, said Ballard. He piled more firewood on.

It was past midnight before she was limber enough to undress. She lay there naked on the mattress with her sallow breasts pooled in the light like wax flowers. Ballard began to dress her in her new clothes.

He sat and brushed her hair with the dimestore brush he'd bought. He undid the top of the lipstick and screwed it out and began to paint her lips.

He would arrange her in different positions and go out and peer in the window at her. After a while he just sat holding her, his hands feeling her body under the new clothes. He undressed her very slowly, talking to her. Then

97

he pulled off his trousers and lay next to her. He spread her loose thighs. You been wantin it, he told her.

Later he hauled her back into the other room. She was loose and not easy to handle. Her bones lay loosely in her flesh. He covered her with the rags and returned to the fire and built it high as it would go and lay in the bed watching it. The flue howled with the enormity of the draw and red flames danced at the chimney top. An enormous brick candle burning in the night. Ballard crammed brush and pieces of stumpwood right up the chimney throat. He made coffee and leaned back on his pallet. Now freeze, you son of a bitch, he told the night beyond the windowpane.

It did. It dropped to six below zero. A brick toppled into the flames. Ballard stoked the fire and pulled his blankets about and composed himself for sleep. It was bright as day in the cabin. He lay staring at the ceiling. Then he got up again and lit the lamp and went into the other room. He turned the girl over and tied the rope around her and ascended into the attic. Again she rose, now naked. Ballard came back down the ladder and took the ladder down and laid it by the wall and went back in and went to bed. Outside the snow fell softly.

HE WOKE IN THE NIGHT with some premonition of ill fate. He sat up. The fire had diminished to a single tongue of flame that stood near motionless from the ashes. He lit the lamp and turned up the wick. A shifting mantle of smoke overhung the room. Thick ribbons of white smoke were seeping down between the boards in the ceiling and he could hear a light crackling noise overhead like something feeding. Oh shit, he said.

He got up, the blanket shawled about his thin and angry shoulders. Through the rives in the boards above him he could see a hellish glow of hot orange. He was pulling on his jacket and shoes. With the rifle in hand he went out into the snow. There in the trampled weedlot he stood looking up at the roof. A crazy-looking gaggle of flames shot up alongside the chimney and subsided again. A rabid crackling from the loft. Clouds of steam were coming off the wet roof and hot pins of light drifted downwind in the blowing snow.

Kiss my goddamned ass, said Ballard. He stood the rifle against a tree and hurried back inside and gathered up his bedding and hauled it out into the snow and dove back in again. He collected his cookware and his little pantry and brought them out and he got the axe and the few tools he owned and what other odds and ends of gear he had stowed in the empty room and flung them into the yard and raced back in and got the ladder and stood it up into the hole and looked up. Huge orange boils of fire were pulsing in the loft. He climbed up the ladder and poked his head through the hole in the ceiling. Instantly he felt his hair singe and crackle. He ducked and patted at his head. Already his eyes were red and weeping from the smoke. He squatted there at the top of the ladder for a few minutes squinting up at the fire and then he climbed back down again.

When he went back outside he had the bears and the tiger in his arms. The roof was now afire. Above the steady roar of it you could hear the old riven oak shakes exploding into flame row on row at the far end of the house with a kind of popping noise. The heat was marvelous.

Ballard stood there in the snow with his jaw hanging. The flames ran down the batboards and up again like burning squirrels. Through the flames of the roof you could see the pinned framing in a row of burning A shapes. Within minutes the cabin was a solid wall of fire. The few panes of glass crackled and fell from their sash in a myriad rupture and the roof dropped with a whooshing noise down into the house. Ballard had to step back, so great the heat was. The snow about the house had begun to draw back leaving a ring of damp ground. After a while the ground began to steam.

Long before morning the house that had kept Ballard from the elements was only a blackened chimney with a pile of smoldering boards at its feet. Ballard crossed the soggy ground and climbed onto the hearth and sat there like an owl. For the warmth of it. He'd long been given to talking to himself but he didn't say a word.

It WAS STILL DARK in the morning when he woke with the cold. He'd piled dead weeds and brush to lay the mattress on and gone to sleep with his feet to the embers of the house, snowflakes falling on him from out of the blackness of the heavens. The snow melted on him and then in the colder hours of morning froze so that he woke beneath a blanket of ice that cracked like glass when he stirred. He hobbled to the hearth in his thin jacket and tried to warm himself. It was still snowing lightly and he knew not what hour it might be.

When he had stopped shivering he got his pan and filled it with snow and set it among the embers. While it was heating he found the axe and cut two poles with which to hang the blanket to dry.

When day came he was sitting in a nest of weeds he'd made on the hearth and he was sipping coffee from a large porcelain cup which he held in both hands. With the advent of this sad gray light he shook the last few drops out of the cup and climbed down from his perch and began to poke through the ashes with a stick. He spent the better part of the morning stirring through the ruins until he was black with woodash to the knees and his hands were black and his face streaked with black where he'd scratched or puzzled. He found not so much as a bone. It was as if she'd never been. Finally he gave it up. He dusted the snow from the remainder of his provisions and fixed himself two baloney sandwiches and squatted in a warm place among the ashes eating them, black fingerprints on the pale bread, eyes dark and huge and vacant.

WITH THE BLANKETLOAD of provisions over his shoulder he looked like some crazy winter gnome clambering up through the snowfilled woods on the side of the mountain. He came on falling and sliding and cursing. It took him an hour to get to the cave. The second trip he carried the axe and the rifle and a lardpail filled with hot coals from the fire at the house.

The entrance to the cave was no more than a crawlway and Ballard was slick with red mud down the front of him from going in and out. Inside there was a large room with a bore of light that climbed slantwise from the red clay floor to a hole in the roof like an incandescent treetrunk. Ballard blew up a flame from wisps of dry grass with his coals and assembled the lamp and lit it and kicked at the remains of an old fire in the center of the cave beneath the roof hole.

He came dragging in slabs of hardwood from the upright shells of dead trees on the mountain and soon he had a good fire going in the cave. When he started back down the mountain for the mattress a steady plume of white smoke was rising from the hole in the ground behind him.

THE WEATHER did not change. Ballard took to wandering over the mountain through the snow to his old homeplace where he'd watch the house, the house's new tenant. He'd go in the night and lie up on the bank and watch him through the kitchen window. Or from the top of the well-house where he could see into the front room where Greer sat before Ballard's very stove with his sockfeet up. Greer wore spectacles and read what looked like seed catalogs. Ballard laid the rifle foresight on his chest. He swung it upward to a spot just above the ear. His finger filled the cold curve of the trigger. Bang, he said.

BALLARD STAMPED the snow from his shoes and leaned his rifle against the side of the house and tapped at the door. He glanced about. The sofa lay mantled in snow and over the snow lay a fine stippling of coalsoot and cat tracks. Behind the house stood the remains of several cars and from the rear glass of one of them a turkey watched him.

The door fell open and the dumpkeeper stood there in his shirtsleeves and suspenders. Come in, Lester, he said.

Ballard entered, his eyes wheeling about, his face stretched in a china smile. But there was no one to see. A young girl was sitting on a car seat holding a baby and when Ballard came in she got up and went into the other room.

Get over here and warm fore ye take your death, said the dumpkeeper, making for the stove.

Where's everbody at? said Ballard.

Shoot, said the dumpkeeper, they've all left out of here.

The mizzes ain't left is she?

Aw naw. She's a visitin her sister and them. Ever one of

the girls is left savin the least'n though. We still got two of the babies here.

How come em to all leave of a sudden like that?

I don't know, said the dumpkeeper. Young people these days, you cain't tell em nothin. You ort to be proud, Lester, that you ain't never married. It is a grief and a heartache and they ain't no reward in it atall. You just raise enemies in ye own house to grow up and cuss ye.

Ballard turned his backside to the stove. Well, he said. I never could see it.

That's where you're smart, said the dumpkeeper.

Ballard agreed mutely, shaking his head.

I heard you got burned out over at your place, the dumpkeeper said.

Plumb to the ground, said Ballard. You never seen such a fire.

What caused it?

I don't know. It started in the attic. I believe it must of been sparks from the chimney.

Was you asleep?

Yeah. I just did get out of there.

What did Waldrop say?

I don't know. I ain't seen him. I ain't lookin for him.

Be proud you wasn't like old man Parton up here got burned down in his bed that time.

Ballard turned around and warmed his hands at the stove. Did they ever find any of him? he said.

WHEN HE GOT TO the head of the hollow he rested, watching behind him the while. The tracks he followed had water standing in them and they went up the mountain but they did not come back down. He lost them later and found some different ones and he spent the afternoon in the woods stalking about like any hunter but when he returned to the cave just short of nightfall with his feet numb in the leaky shoes he had not found any of the whiskey and he had not seen Kirby.

He ran into Greer the next morning. It had begun to rain, a small cold winter rain that Ballard cursed. He lowered his head and tucked the rifle under his arm and stepped to one side to pass but the other would not have it so.

Howdy, he said.

Howdy, said Ballard.

You're Ballard ain't ye?

Ballard did not raise his head. He was watching the man's

shoes there in the wet leaves of the overgrown logging road. He said: No, I ain't him, and went on.


LORD THEY caught me, Lester, said Kirby.

Caught ye?

I'm on three year probation.

Ballard stared around the little room with its linoleum floor and cheap furniture. Well kiss my ass, he said.

Ain't it a bitch? I never thought about them bein niggers.

Niggers?

They sent niggers. That's who I sold to. Sold to em three times. One of em set right there in that chair and drunk a pint. Drunk it and got up and walked out and got in the car. I don't see how he done it. He might of drove for all I know. They caught everbody. Got old lady Bright up in Cocke County even and she's been sellin whiskey non stop since fore I was born.

Ballard leaned and spat into a can sitting in the floor. Well fuck it, he said.

I sure would of never thought about them sendin niggers, said Kirby.

BALLARD STOOD AT the door. There was no car in the driveway. A pale yellow trapezoid of light lay in the mud beneath the window. Within, the idiot child crawled in the floor and the girl was curled on the sofa reading a magazine. He raised his hand and tapped.

When the door opened he was standing there already wearing his sickish smile, his lips dry and tight over his teeth. Hidy, he said.

He ain't here, said the girl. She stood hiploose in the doorframe and regarded him with frank indifference.

What time you expect him?

I don't know. He's took Mama to church. They won't be back fore ten-thirty or eleven.

Well, said Ballard.

She said nothing.

Turned off cool, ain't it?

It is standin here with the door open.

Well ain't you goin to ast me in for a minute.

She thought about it before she swung the door back. You could see it in her eyes. But she let him in, more's the fool.

He entered shuffling, beating his hands together. How's that big boy? he said.

He's crazy as ever, she said, headed for the sofa and her magazine.

Ballard squatted before the stained and drooling cretin and tousled its near bald head. Why that boy's got good sense, he said. Ain't ye?

Shoot, said the girl.

Ballard eyed her. She was wearing pink slacks of cheap cotton and she sat in the sofa with her legs crossed under her and a pillow in her lap. He rose and went to the stove and stood with his back to it. The stove was enclosed waist-high in a chickenwire fence. The posts were toenailed to the floor and the fencing was nailed down as well. I bet he could push this over if he wanted to, said Ballard.

I'd smack the fire out of him too, said the girl.

Ballard was watching her. He narrowed his eyes cunningly and smiled. He's yourn, ain't he? he said.

The girl's face snapped up. You're crazy as shit, she said.

Ballard leered. Steam sifted up from his dark trouserlegs. You cain't fool me, he said.

You're a liar, the girl said.

You wisht I was.

You better hush.

Ballard turned to warm his front side. A car passed in the road. They both craned their necks to follow the lights along.

She turned back and saw him and made a chickennecked grimace to mock him. The child in the floor sat drooling nor had it moved.

Wouldn't be that old crazy Thomas boy, would it? said Ballard.

The girl glared at him. Her face was flushed and her eyes red.

You ain't slipped off in the bushes with that old crazy thing have ye?

You better shut your mouth, Lester Ballard. I'll tell Daddy on you.

I'll tell Daddy on you, whined Ballard.

You just wait and see if I don't.

Shoot, said Ballard. I was just teasin ye.

Why don't you go on.

I guess you too young to know when a man's teasin ye.

You ain't even a man. You're just a crazy thing.

I might be more than you think, said Ballard. How come you wear them britches?

What's it to you?

Ballard's mouth was dry. You cain't see nothin, he said.

She looked at him blankly, then she reddened. I ain't got nothin for you to see, she said.

Ballard took a few wooden steps toward the sofa and then stopped in the middle of the floor. Why don't you show me them nice titties, he said hoarsely.

She stood up and pointed at the door. You get out of here, she said. Right now.

Come on, Ballard wheezed. I won't ast ye nothin else.

Lester Ballard, when Daddy comes home he's goin to kill you. Now I said get out of here and I mean it. She stamped her foot.

Ballard looked at her. All right, he said. If that's the way you want it. He went to the door and opened it and went out and shut the door behind him. He heard her latch it. The night out there was clear and cold and the moon sat in a great ring in the sky. Ballard's breath rose whitely toward the dark of the heavens. He turned and looked back at the house. She was watching from the corner of the window. He went on down the broken driveway to the road and crossed the ditch and went along the edge of the yard and crossed back up to the house. He picked up the rifle where he'd left it leaning against a crabapple tree and he went along the side of the house and stepped up onto a low wall of cinder block and went along it past the clothes-line and the coalpile to where he could see in the window there. He could see the back of her head above the sofa. He watched her for a while and then he raised the rifle and cocked it and laid the sights on her head. He had just done this when suddenly she rose from the sofa and turned facing the window. Ballard fired.

The crack of the rifle was outrageously loud in the cold silence. Through the spidered glass he saw her slouch and stand again. He levered another shell into the chamber and raised the rifle and then she fell. He reached down and scrabbled about in the frozen mud for the empty shell but he could not find it. He raced around the house to the front and mounted the spindly steps and came up short against the door. You dumb son of a bitch, he said. You heard her lock it. He leaped to the ground and ran to the back of the house and entered a low screened porch and pushed open the kitchen door and went through and into the front room. She was lying in the floor but she was not dead. She was moving. She seemed to be trying to get up. A thin stream of blood ran aross the yellow linoleum rug and seeped away darkly in the wood of the floor. Ballard gripped the rifle and watched her. Die, goddamn you, he said. She did.

When she had ceased moving he went about the room gathering up newspapers and magazines and shredding them. The idiot watched mutely. Ballard ripped away the chickenwire from around the stove and pushed the stove over with his foot. The pipe crashed into the room in a cloud of coalsoot. He snatched open the stove door and hot embers rolled out. He piled on papers. Soon a fire going in the middle of the room. Ballard raised up the dead girl. She was slick with blood. He got her onto his shoulder and looked around. The rifle. It was leaning against the sofa. He got it and looked about wildly. Already the ceiling of the room was packed with seething tiers of smoke and small fires licked along the bare wood floor at the edge of the linoleum. As he whirled about there in the kitchen door the last thing he saw through the smoke was the idiot child. It sat watching him, berryeyed filthy and frightless among the painted flames.

BALLARD WAS WALKING the road near the top of the mountain when the sheriff pulled up behind him in the car. The sheriff told Ballard to put the rifle down but Ballard didn't move. He stood there by the side of the road straight up and down with the rifle in one hand and he didn't even turn around to see who'd spoke. The sheriff reached his pistol out the window and cocked it. You could hear very clearly in the cold air the click of the hammer and the click of the hand dropping into the cylinder locking notch. Boy, you better stick it in the ground, the sheriff said.

Ballard stood the butt of the rifle in the road and let go of it. It fell into the roadside bushes.

Turn around.

Now come over here.

Now just stand there a minute.

Now get in here.

Now hold your hands out.

If you leave my rifle there somebody's goin to get it.

I'll worry about your goddamned rifle.

THE MAN BEHIND the desk had folded his hands in front of him as if about to pray. He gazed at Ballard across the tips of his fingers. Well, he said, if you hadn't done anything wrong what were you scoutin the bushes for that nobody could find you?

I know how they do ye, Ballard muttered. Thow ye in jail and beat the shit out of ye.

This man ever been mistreated down here, Sheriff?

He knows better than that.

They tell me you cussed deputy Walker.

Well did you?

What are you lookin over there for?

I was just lookin.

Mr Walker's not goin to tell you what to say.

He might tell me what not to.

Is it true that you burned down Mr Waldrop's house?

No.

You were living in it at the time that it burned.

That's a . . . I wasn't done it. I'd left out of there a long time fore that.

It was quiet in the room. After a while the man behind the desk lowered his hands and folded them in his lap. Mr Ballard, he said. You are either going to have to find some other way to live or some other place in the world to do it in.

BALLARD ENTERED the store and slammed the iron barred door behind him. The store was empty save for Mr Fox who nodded to this small and harried looking customer. The customer did not nod back. He went along the shelves picking and choosing among the goods, the cans all marshaled with their labels to the front, wrenching holes in their ordered rows and stacking them on the counter in front of the storekeeper. Finally he fetched up in front of the meatcase. Mr Fox rose and donned a white apron, old bloodstains bleached light pink, tied it in the back and approached the meatcase and switched on a light that illuminated rolls of baloney and rounds of cheese and a tray of thin sliced pork chops among the sausages and sousemeat.

Slice me about a half pound of that there baloney, said Ballard.

Mr Fox fetched it out and laid it on the butcher block and took up a knife and began to pare away thin slices. These he doled up one at a time onto a piece of butcher-paper. When he had done he laid down the knife and placed the paper in the scales. He and Ballard watched the needle swing. What else now, said the storekeeper, tying up the package of meat with a string.

Give me some of that there cheese.

He bought a sack of cigarette tobacco and stood there rolling a smoke and nodding at the groceries. Add them up, he said.

The storekeeper figured the merchandise on his scratch-pad, sliding the goods from one side of the counter to the other as he went. He raised up and pushed his glasses back with his thumb.

Five dollars and ten cents, he said.

Just put it on the stob for me.

Ballard, when are you goin to pay me?

Well. I can give ye some on it today.

How much on it.

Well. Say three dollars.

The storekeeper was figuring on his pad.

How much do I owe altogether? said Ballard.

Thirty-four dollars and nineteen cents.

Includin this here?

Includin this here.

Well let me just give ye the four dollars and nineteen cents and that'll leave it thirty even.

The storekeeper looked at Ballard. Ballard, he said, how old are you?

Twenty-seven if it's any of your business.

Twenty-seven. And in twenty-seven years you've managed to accumulate four dollars and nineteen cents?

The storekeeper was figuring on his pad.

Ballard waited. What are you figurin? he asked suspiciously.

Just a minute, said the storekeeper. After a while he raised the pad up and squinted at it. Well, he said. Accordin to my figures, at this rate it's goin to take a hundred and ninety-four years to pay out the thirty dollars. Ballard, I'm sixty-seven now.

Why that's crazy.

Of course this is figured if you don't buy nothin else.

Why that's crazier'n hell.

Well, I could of made a mistake in the figures. Did you want to check em?

Ballard pushed at the scratchpad the storekeeper was offering him. I don't want to see that, he said.

Well, what I think I'm goin to do along in here is just try to minimize my losses. So if you've got four dollars and nineteen cents why don't you just get four dollars and nineteen cents' worth of groceries.

Ballard's face was twitching.

What did you want to put back? said the storekeeper.

I ain't puttin a goddamn thing back, said Ballard, laying out the five dollars and slapping down the dime.

BALLARD CROSSED the mountain into Blount County one Sunday morning in the early part of February. There is a spring on the side of the mountain that runs from solid stone. Kneeling in the snow among the fairy tracks of birds and deermice Ballard leaned his face to the green water and drank and studied his dishing visage in the pool. He halfway put his hand to the water as if he would touch the face that watched there but then he rose and wiped his mouth and went on through the woods.

Old woods and deep. At one time in the world there were woods that no one owned and these were like them. He passed a windfelled tulip poplar on the mountainside that held aloft in the grip of its roots two stones the size of fieldwagons, great tablets on which was writ only a tale of vanished seas with ancient shells in cameo and fishes etched in lime. Ballard among gothic treeboles, almost jaunty in the outsized clothing he wore, fording drifts of kneedeep snow, going along the south face of a limestone bluff beneath which birds scratching in the bare earth paused to watch.

The road when he reached it was unmarked by any track at all. Ballard descended into it and went on. It was almost noon and the sun was very bright on the snow and the snow shone with a myriad crystal incandescence. The shrouded road wound off before him almost lost among the trees and a stream ran beside the road, dark under bowers of ice, small glass-fanged caverns beneath tree roots where the water sucked unseen. In the frozen roadside weeds were coiled white ribbons of frost, you'd never figure how they came to be. Ballard ate one as he went, the rifle on his shoulder, his feet enormous with snow where it clung to the sacks with which he'd wrapped them.

By and by he came upon a house, silent in the silent landscape, a rough scarf of smoke unwinding upward from the chimney. There were tire tracks in the road but they had been snowed over in the night. Ballard came on down the mountain past more houses and past the ruins of a tannery into a road freshly traveled, the corded tracks of tirechains curving away into the white woods and a jade river curving away toward the mountains to the south.

When he got to the store he sat on a box on the porch and with his pocketknife cut the twine that bound his legs and feet and took off the sacks and shook them out and laid them on the box with the pieces of twine and stood up. He was wearing black lowcut shoes that were longer than he should have needed. The rifle he'd left under the bridge as he crossed the river. He stamped his feet and opened the door and went in.

A group of men and boys were gathered about the stove and they stopped talking when Ballard entered. Ballard went to the back of the stove, nodding slightly to the store's inhabitants. He held his hands to the heat and looked casually about. Cold enough for ye'ns? he said.

Nobody said if it was or wasn't. Ballard coughed and rubbed his hands together and crossed to the drink box and got an orange drink and opened it and got a cake and paid at the counter. The storekeeper dropped the dime into the till and shut the drawer. He said: It's a sight in the world of snow, ain't it?

Ballard agreed that it was, leaning on the counter, eating the cake and taking small sips from the drink. After a while he leaned toward the storekeeper. You ain't needin a watch are ye? he said.

What? said the storekeeper.

A watch. Did you need a watch.

The storekeeper looked at Ballard blankly. A watch? he said. What kind of a watch?

I got different kinds. Here. Ballard setting down his drink and half-eaten cake on the counter and reaching into his pockets. He pulled forth three wristwatches and laid them out. The storekeeper poked at them once or twice with his finger. I don't need no watch, he said. I got some in the counter yonder been there a year.

Ballard looked where he was pointing. A few dusty

watches in cellophane packets among the socks and hair-nets.

What do you get for yourn? he asked.

Eight dollars.

Ballard eyed the merchant's watches doubtfully. Well, he said. He finished the cake and took up his own watches by their straps and took his drink and crossed the floor to the stove again. He held the watches out, tendering them uncertainly at the man nearest him. You all don't need a wristwatch do ye? he said.

The man glanced at the watches and glanced away.

Let's see em over here, old buddy, said a fat boy by the stove.

Ballard handed the watches across.

What do ye want for em?

I thought I'd get five dollars.

What, for all three of em?

Why hell no. Five dollars each.

Shit.

Let's see thatn, Orvis.

Wait a minute, I'm look in at it.

Let's see it.

That there's a good watch.

Let me have it. What will ye take for thisn?

Five dollar.

I'll give two and won't ast ye where ye got it.

I cain't do it.

Let me see that othern, Fred. What's wrong with em?

Ain't a damn thing wrong with em. You hear em runnin don't ye?

I'll give you three for that there gold lookin one.

Ballard looked from one to the other of them. I'll take four, he said, and pick your choice.

What'll ye take for all of em?

Ballard totted figures in the air for a moment. Twelve dollars, he said.

Why hell, that ain't no deal. Don't ye get a discount on job lots?

Is them all the watches you got?

Just them three is all.

Here. Hand him thesens back.

Ain't you goin to get in the watch business today, Orvis?

I cain't get my jobber to come down.

What'll you give for em? said Ballard.

I'll give eight dollars for the three of em.

Ballard looked about at the men. They were watching him to see what price used watches would bring this Sunday morning. He weighed the watches in his hand a moment and handed them across. You bought em, he said.

The watchbuyer rose and handed across the money and took the watches. You want thisn for three? he said to the man next to him.

Yeah, let me have it.

Anybody else want one for three? He held up the spare watch.

The other man who had been looking at the watches

straightened out his leg across the floor and reached into his pocket. I'll take if off of ye, he said.

What'll ye take for thatn you got, Orvis?

Might take five.

Shit. You ain't got but two in it.

This here's a good watch.


WHEN BALLARD reached the river he looked about the empty white countryside and then dropped down off the road and under the bridge. Coming up the river were tracks not his own. Ballard scrambled up under the stanchions and reached up to the beam atop which he'd left the rifle. There for a moment he flailed wildly, his hand scrabbling along the concrete, his eye to the river and the tracks there which already he was trailing to the end of his life. Then his hand closed upon the stock of the rifle. He fetched it down, cursing, his heart hammering. You'd try it, wouldn't ye? he wailed at the tracks in the snow. His voice beneath the arches of the bridge came back hollow and alien and Ballard listened to the echo of it with his head tilted like a dog and then he climbed the bank and started back up the road.

IT WAS DARK WHEN he reached the cave. He crawled through and lit a match and got the lamp and lit it and set it by the ring of stones that marked the firepit. The nearer walls of the cavern composed themselves out of the constant night with their pale stone drapery folds and a faultline in the vault's ceiling appeared with a row of dripping limestone teeth. In the black smokehole overhead the remote and lidless stars of the Pleiades burned cold and absolute. Ballard kicked at the fire and turned a few dull cherry coals up out of the ash and bones. He fetched dry grass and twigs and lit the fire and went back out with his pan and brought it in filled with snow and set it by the fire. His mattress lay in a pile of brush with the stuffed animals upon it and his other few possessions lay about in the grotto where chance had arranged them.

When he had the fire going he took his flashlight and went across the room and disappeared down a narrow passageway.

Ballard made his way by damp stone corridors down inside the mountain to another room. Here his light scudded across a growth of limestone columns and what looked like huge stone urns moist and illshapen. From the floor of the room an underground stream rose. It welled up blackly in a calcite basin and flowed down a narrow aqueduct where the room tailed off through a black hole. Ballard's light glanced from the surface of the pool unaltered, as if bent back by some strange underground force. Everywhere water dripped and spattered and the wet cave walls looked waxed or lacquered in the beam of light.

He crossed the room and followed the stream out and down the narrow gorge through which it flowed, the water rushing off into the darkness before him, descending from pool to pool in stone cups of its own devising and Ballard nimble over the rocks and along a ledge, keeping his feet dry, straddling the watercourse at points, his light picking out on the pale stone floor of the stream white crawfish that backed and turned blindly.

He followed this course for perhaps a mile down all its turnings and through narrows that fetched him sideways advancing like a fencer and through a tunnel that brought him to his belly, the smell of the water beside him in the trough rich with minerals and past the chalken dung of he knew not what animals until he climbed up a chimney to a corridor above the stream and entered into a tall and bellshaped cavern. Here the walls with their softlooking convolutions, slavered over as they were with wet and bloodred mud, had an organic look to them, like the innards of some great beast. Here in the bowels of the mountain Ballard turned his light on ledges or pallets of stone where dead people lay like saints.

A WINTER dreadful cold it was. He thought before it was over that he would look like one of the bitter spruces that grew slant downwind out of the shale and lichens on the hogback. Coming up the mountain through the blue winter twilight among great boulders and the ruins of giant trees prone in the forest he wondered at such upheaval. Disorder in the woods, trees down, new paths needed. Given charge Ballard would have made things more orderly in the woods and in men's souls.

It snowed again. It snowed for four days and when Ballard went down the mountain again it took him the best part of the morning to cross to the ridge above Greer's place. There he could hear the chuck of an axe muted with distance and snowfall. He could see nothing. The snow was gray against the sky, soft on his lashes. It fell without a sound. Ballard cradled the rifle in his arm and made his way down the slope toward the house.

He crouched behind the barn listening for sound of

Greer. There in the frozen mire of mud and dung deeply plugged with hoofprints. When he came through the barn it was empty. The loft was filled with hay. Ballard stood in the forebay door looking down through the falling snow at the gray shape of the house. He crossed to the chicken house and undid the wire that held the hasp and entered. A few white hens eyed him nervously from their cubbynests on the far wall. Ballard passed along a row of roosting rails and went through a chickenwire door to the feedroom. There he loaded his pockets with shelled corn and came back. He surveyed the hens, clucked his tongue at them and reached for one. It erupted from the box with a long squawk and flapped past and lit in the floor and trotted off. Ballard cursed. In the uproar the other hens were following by ones and pairs. He lunged and grabbed one by the tail as it came soaring out. It set up an outraged shrieking until Ballard could get it by the neck. Holding the struggling bird in both hands and with his rifle between his knees he crowhopped to the small dustwebbed window and peered out. Nothing stirred. You son of a bitch, said Ballard, to the chicken or Greer or both. He wrung the hen's neck and went quickly through the nesting boxes gathering up the few eggs and putting them in his pockets and then he went out again.

IN THE SPRING or warmer weather when the snow thaws in the woods the tracks of winter reappear on slender pedestals and the snow reveals in palimpsest old buried wanderings, struggles, scenes of death. Tales of winter brought to light again like time turned back upon itself. Ballard went through the woods kicking down his old trails where they veered over the hill toward his onetime homeplace. Old comings and goings. The tracks of a fox raised out of the snow intaglio like little mushrooms and berrystains where birds shat crimson mutes upon the snow like blood.

When he reached the overlook he stood his rifle against the stones and watched the house below him. There was no smoke coming from the chimney. Ballard watched with his arms folded. He asked Greer where he was today. A gray and colder day with all the melting snow ceased from its dripping and runneling. Ballard watched the first flakes fall like ash into the valley.

Where are you, you bastard? he called.

Two minute doilies of snow settled and perished on the crossed arms of his coat. He watched until the silent house grew dim below him in the gray snowfall. After a while he took up the rifle once again and crossed the ridge to where he could see the road. There was nobody going up or down. Already the snow was falling so that you could not see up the valley at all. A spray of small birds came out of the snowfall and passed like windblown leaves into the silence again. Ballard crouched on his heels with the rifle between his knees. He told the snow to fall faster and it did.

AFTER THE SNOW ceased he went every day. He'd watch from his half mile promontory, see Greer come from the house for wood or go to the barn or to the chicken house. After he'd gone in again Ballard would wander about aimlessly in the woods talking to himself. He laid queer plans. His shuffling boot tracks trampling out the prints of lesser life. Where mice had gone, or foxes hunting in the night. The dovelike imprimatur of a stooping owl.

He'd long been wearing the underclothes of his female victims but now he took to appearing in their outerwear as well. A gothic doll in illfit clothes, its carmine mouth floating detached and bright in the white landscape. Down there the valley with the few ruststained roofs and faintest wisps of smoke. The ribboned slash of mud that the road made up the white valley and beyond it the fold on fold of mountains with their black weirs of winter treelimbs and dull green cedars.

His own tracks came from the cave bloodred with cave-mud and paled across the slope as if the snow had cauterized his feet until he left dry white prints in the snow. False spring came again with a warm wind. The snow melted off into little patches of gray ice among the wet leaves. With the advent of this weather bats began to stir from somewhere deep in the cave. Ballard lying on his pallet by the fire one evening saw them come from the dark of the tunnel and ascend through the hole overhead fluttering wildly in the ash and smoke like souls rising from hades. When they were gone he watched the hordes of cold stars sprawled across the smokehole and wondered what stuff they were made of, or himself.

III

YONDER IT IS, Sheriff, said the sheriffs deputy.

All right. Go on to the top and turn around.

They drove on up the deeply mired road fishtailing slightly and unreeling long slabs of wet mud from under the tires until they came to the loop at the end of the road. Coming back down you could see the ruts where they went off into the weeds and you could see where the young trees were crushed and where the tiretracks went on down the side of the mountain.

Yonder she lays, said the deputy.

The car was turned on its side in a deep ravine some hundred feet below them. The sheriff wasn't looking at it. He was looking back up the road toward the turnaround. I wisht we'd of been here three days ago when they was still some snow on the ground, he said. Let's go down and look at it.

They stood on the side of the car and raised the door up

and the deputy descended into the interior. After a while he said: They ain't a damn thing in here, Sheriff.

What about in the glovebox?

Not a thing.

Look up in under the seats.

I done looked.

Look some more.

When he came up out of the car he had a bottlecap in his hand. He handed it to the sheriff.

What's that? said the sheriff.

That's it.

The sheriff looked at the bottlecap. Let's get the turtle-deck open, he said.

In the trunk was a spare tire and a jack and a lugwrench and some rags and two empty bottles. The sheriff was standing with his hands in his pockets looking back up the side of the ravine toward the road. If you wanted to get from here to the road, he said—which you would if you was here—how would you go?

The deputy pointed. I'd go right up that there gully, he said.

So would I, said the sheriff.

Where do you reckon he went?

I don't know.

How long did you say his old lady says he's been gone?

Since Sunday evenin.

They sure the girl was with him?

So they say. They was engaged.

Maybe they took off through the woods or somethin.

They wasn't in the car, the sheriff said.

They wasn't?

No.

Well how did it get here?

I believe somebody's shoved it off in here.

Well maybe they run off together. Might better find out how much he owed on the car. That could be what . . .

I done have. It's paid for.

The deputy nudged a few small stones with the toe of his boot. After a while he looked up. Well, he said. Where do you reckon they've got to?

I reckon they've got to wherever that gal got to that was supposed to be with that boy we found up here.

She was supposed to of been goin with that Blalock boy we talked to.

Yeah, well. These young people keep pretty active some of em. Let's go up here.

They walked up the road to the turnaround. On the far side they found shoetracks in the mud along the edge of the road. Further down the circle they found more. The sheriff just sort of nodded at them.

What do you reckon, Sheriff? said the deputy.

Why nothin. It could just be where somebody got out to piss. He was looking off down the road. Do you reckon, he said, that if you was to shove a car off from along in here it might get as far as where we're parked down yonder fore it left the road?

The deputy looked with him. Well, he said. It's possible. I'd say it might could.

So would I, said the sheriff.

BALLARD'S NEW SHOES sucked in the mud as he approached the pickup truck. He had the rifle under his arm and the flashlight in his hand. When he got to the truck he opened the door and flicked the light on and trapped in its yellow beam the white faces of a boy and a girl in each other's arms.

The girl was the first to speak. She said: He's got a gun.

Ballard's head was numb. They seemed assembled there the three of them for some purpose other than his. He said: Let's see your driver's license.

You ain't the law, the boy said.

I'll be the judge of that, said Ballard. What are you all doin up here?

We was just settin here, the girl said. She wore a sprig of gauze ferns at her shoulder with two roses of burgundy crepe.

You was fixin to screw, wasn't ye? He watched their faces.

You better watch your mouth, the boy said.

You want to make me?

You put down that rifle and I will.

Any time you feel froggy, jump, said Ballard.

The boy reached to the dashboard and turned on the ignition and began to crank the engine.

Quit it, said Ballard.

The engine did not start. The boy had raised his hand as if he would bat at the riflebarrel when Ballard shot him through the neck. He fell sideways into the girl's lap. She folded her hands and put them under her chin. Oh no, she said.

Ballard levered another shell into the chamber. I told that fool, he said. Didn't I tell him? I don't know why people don't want to listen.

The girl looked at the boy and then she looked up at Ballard. She was holding her hands in the air as if she didn't know where to put them. She said: What did you have to go and do that for?

It was up to him, said Ballard. I told the idjit.

Oh god, said the girl.

You better get out of there.

What?

Out. Come on out of there.

What are you goin to do?

That's for me to know and you to find out.

The girl pushed the boy from her and slid across the seat and stepped out into the mud of the road.

Turn around, Ballard said.

What are you goin to do?

Just turn around and never mind.

I have to go to the bathroom, the girl said.

You don't need to worry about that, said Ballard.

Turning her by the shoulder he laid the muzzle of the rifle at the base of her skull and fired.

She dropped as if the bones in her body had been liquefied. Ballard tried to catch her but she slumped into the mud. He got hold of her dress by the nape to raise her but the material parted in his fist and in the end he had to stand the rifle against the fender of the truck and take her under the arms.

He dragged her through the weeds, walking backwards, watching over his shoulder. Her head was lolling and blood ran down her neck and Ballard had dragged her out of her shoes. He was breathing harshly and his eyeballs were wild and white. He laid her down in the woods not fifty feet from the road and threw himself on her, kissing the still warm mouth and feeling under her clothes. Suddenly he stopped and raised up. He lifted her skirt and looked down at her. She had wet herself. He cursed and pulled down the panties and dabbed at the pale thighs with the hem of the girl's skirt. He had his trousers about his knees when he heard the truck start.

The sound he made was not unlike the girl's. A dry sucking of air, mute with terror. He leaped up hauling at his breeches and tore through the brush toward the road.

A crazed mountain troll clutching up a pair of blood-stained breeches by one hand and calling out in a high mad gibbering, bursting from the woods and hurtling down the gravel road behind a lightless truck receding half obscured in rising dust. He pounded down the mountain till he could run no more nor had he breath to call after. Before long he had stopped to buckle his belt and he went lurching on, holding his side, slumped and breathing hard and saying to himself: You won't get far, you dead son of a bitch. He was halfway down the mountain before he realized he did not have the rifle. He stopped. Then he went on anyway.

When he came out on the valley road he looked down toward the highway. The road in the moonlight lay beneath a lightly sustained trail of dust like a river under a mantle of mist and for as far as he could see. Ballard's heart lay in his chest like a stone. He squatted in the dust of the road until his breathing eased. Then he rose and started back up the mountain again. He tried to run at first but he could not. It took him almost an hour to make the three miles back to the top.

He found the rifle where it had fallen from the truck fender and he checked it and then went on into the woods. She was lying as he had left her and she was cold and wooden with death. Ballard howled curses until he was choking and then he knelt and worked her around onto his shoulders and struggled up. Scuttling down the mountain with the thing on his back he looked like a man beset by some ghast succubus, the dead girl riding him with legs bowed akimbo like a monstrous frog.

BALLARD WATCHED THEM from the saddle in the mountain, a small thing brooding there, squatting with the rifle in his arms. It had been raining for three days. The creek far below him out of its banks, the fields flooded, sheets of standing water spotted with winter weeds and fodder. Ballard's hair hung from his thin skull in lank wet strings and gray water dripped from his hair and from the end of his nose.

In the night the side of the mountain winked with lamps and torches. Late winter revelers among the trees or some like hunters calling each to each there in the dark. In the dark Ballard passed beneath them, scuttling with his ragged chattel down stone tunnels within the mountain.

Toward dawn he emerged from a hole in a rock on the far side of the mountain and peered about like a groundhog before commiting himself to the gray and rainy daylight. With his rifle in one hand and his blanketload of gear he set off through the thin woods toward the cleared land beyond.

He crossed a fence into a half flooded field and made his way toward the creek. At the ford it was more than twice its right width. Ballard studied the water and moved on downstream. After a while he was back. The creek was totally opaque, a thick and brickcolored medium that hissed in the reeds. As he watched a drowned sow shot into the ford and spun slowly with pink and bloated dugs and went on. Ballard stashed the blanket in a stand of sedge and returned to the cave.

When he got back to the creek it seemed to have run yet higher. He carried a crate of odd miscellany, men's and ladies' clothes, the three enormous stuffed toys streaked with mud. Adding to this load the rifle and the blanketful of things he'd carried down he stepped into the water.

The creek climbed his legs in wild batwings. Ballard tottered and rebalanced and took a second grip on his load and went on. Before he even reached the creekbed he was wading kneedeep. When it reached his waist he began to curse aloud. A vitriolic invocation for the receding of the waters. Anyone watching him could have seen he would not turn back if the creek swallowed him under. It did. He was in fast water to his chest, struggling along on tiptoe gingerly and leaning upstream when a log came steaming into the flat. He saw it coming and began to curse. It spun broadside to him and it came on with something of animate ill will. Git, he screamed at it, a hoarse croak in the roar of the water. It came on bobbing and bearing in its perimeter a meniscus of pale brown froth in which floated walnuts, twigs, a slender bottle neck erect and tilting like a metronome.

Git, goddamn it. Ballard shoved at the log with the barrel of the rifle. It swung down upon him in a rush and he hooked his rifle arm over it. The crate capsized and floated off. Ballard and the log bore on into the rapids below the ford and Ballard was lost in a pandemonium of noises, the rifle aloft in one arm now like some demented hero or bedraggled parody of a patriotic poster come aswamp and his mouth wide for the howling of oaths until the log swept into a deeper pool and rolled and the waters closed over him.

He came up flailing and sputtering and began to thrash his way toward the line of willows that marked the sub-merged creek bank. He could not swim, but how would you drown him? His wrath seemed to buoy him up. Some halt in the way of things seems to work here. See him. You could say that he's sustained by his fellow men, like you. Has peopled the shore with them calling to him. A race that gives suck to the maimed and the crazed, that wants their wrong blood in its history and will have it. But they want this man's life. He has heard them in the night seeking him with lanterns and cries of execration. How then is he borne up? Or rather, why will not these waters take him?

When he reached the willows he pulled himself up and found that he stood in scarcely a foot of water. There he turned and shook the rifle alternately at the flooded creek and at the gray sky out of which the rain still fell grayly and without relent and the curses that hailed up above the thunder of the water carried to the mountain and back like echoes from the clefts of bedlam.

He splashed his way to high ground and began to unload and disassemble the rifle, putting the shells in his shirtpocket and wiping the water from the gun with his forefinger and blowing through the barrel, muttering to himself the while. He took out the shells and dried them the best he could and reloaded the rifle and levered a shell into the chamber. Then he started downstream at a trot.

The only thing that he recovered was the crate and it was empty. Once far downstream he thought he saw toy bears bobbing on the spate but they were lost from sight beyond a stand of trees and he was already nearer the highway than he wished and so turned back.

Ultimately he crossed higher in the mountains. A steep and black ravine in which a wild torrent sang. Ballard on a mossbacked footlog bent beneath his sodden mudstained mattress went with care, holding the rifle before him. How white the water was, how constant its form in the speeding flumes below. How black the rocks.

When he reached the sinkhole on the mountain the mattress was so heavy with rainwater that it staggered him. He crawled through a hole in the stone wall of the sink and pulled the mattress in after him.

All that night he hauled his possessions and all night long it rained. When he dragged the last rancid mold-crept corpse through the wall of the sinkhole and down the dark and dripping corridor daylight had already broached a pale gray band in the weeping sky eastward. His track through the black leaves of the forest with the drag marks of heels looked like a small wagon had passed there. In the night it had frozen and he came up through a field of grass webbed with little panes of ice and into a wood where the trees were seized in ice each twig like small black bones in glass that cried or shattered in the wind. Ballard's trousercuffs had frozen into two drums that clattered at his ankles and in the shoes he wore his toes lay cold and bloodless. He walked out from the sinkhole to see the day, nearly sobbing with exhaustion. Nothing moved in that dead and fabled waste, the woods garlanded with frostflowers, weeds spiring up from white crystal fantasies like the stone lace in a cave's floor. He had not stopped cursing. Whatever voice spoke him was no demon but some old shed self that came yet from time to time in the name of sanity, a hand to gentle him back from the rim of his disastrous wrath.

He built a fire in the floor of the cave by a running stream. Smoke gathered in the dome above and seeped slowly up through myriad fissures and pores and rose in a stygian mist through the dripping woods. When he tried the action of the rifle it was frozen fast. He knelt on the barrel and grappled with it, tearing at the lever with his hands. When it did not give he threw it into the fire. But fetched it out again and stood it against the wall before it had suffered more than a scorched forestock. He crushed wild chicory into the blackened coffeepot and dipped the pot full of water. It simmered and hissed and sang in the flames. Ballard's shadow veering dark and mutant over the cupped stone walls. He brought out a pan of cornbread partly eaten and set it by the fire where the dry crusts lay curled like clayshards in a summer gully.

In the black midday he woke half frozen and mended up the fire. Hot pains were rifling through his feet. He lay back down. The water in the mattress had soaked through to his back and he lay there shivering with his arms crossed at his chest and after a while he slept again.

When he woke it was to agony. He sat up and gripped his feet. He howled aloud. With gingery steps he crossed the stone floor to the water and sat and put his feet in. The creek felt hot. He sat there soaking his feet and gibbering, a sound not quite crying that echoed from the walls of the grotto like the mutterings of a band of sympathetic apes.

THE HIGH SHERIFF of Sevier County came down the courthouse steps as far as the last stone above the flooded lawn and gazed out over the water where it lay flat and gray and choked with debris, stretching in quiet canals up the streets and alleys, the tops of the parking meters just visible and off to the left the faintest suggestion of movement, a dull sluggish wrinkling where the mainstream of the Little Pigeon river tugged at the standing water in the flats. When the deputy came rowing across the lawn in the skiff the sheriff watched him with slowly shaking head. The deputy swung the rear of the skiff about and backoared until the transom banged against the stone landing.

Cotton, you a hell of a oarsman.

You goddamn right.

Where the hell you been?

The oarsman stayed the oars, the boat dipped heavily.

You goin to ride standin up like Napoleon? Reason I'm late I had to give Bill Scruggs a ticket.

A ticket?

Yeah. I caught him goin up Bruce Street speedin in a motorboat.

Horseshit.

The deputy grinned and dipped the oars. Ain't this the goddamnedest thing ever you seen? he said.

Rain drizzled lightly. The sheriff peered out at the flooded town from under his dripping hatbrim. You ain't seen a old man with a long beard buildin a great big boat anywheres have ye? he said.

They rowed up the main street of the town past flooded shops and small cafes. Two men came from a store with a rowboat piled with stained boxes and loose mounds of clothing. One oared the boat, one waded behind.

Mornin Sheriff, called out the man in the water, raising his hand.

Mornin Ed, said the sheriff.

The man in the boat gestured with his chin.

Did Mr Parker see you? said the man in the water.

We're just goin up there now.

Seems like trouble ought to make people closer stead of some tryin to rob others.

Some people you cain't do nothin with, the sheriff said.

Ain't that the truth.

They rowed on. Take care, said the sheriff.

Right, said the man in the water.

They rowed into the hardware store entranceway and the

deputy shipped the oars. Inside by lamplight people were moving about sloshing heavily through the water. A man climbed into the showcase window and peered out at the sheriff through the broken glass.

Howdy Fate, he said.

Howdy Eustis.

Biggest thing they took was guns.

That's what they take.

I don't even know how many. I expect we'll find stuff missin for a year.

Can you get the numbers on em?

Not till the waters recede. If they ever do. The inventory sheets are in the basement.

Well.

It's supposed to clear tomorrow. Although at this point I really don't give a shit. Do you?

It's the worst I ever saw in my time, the sheriff said.

It was supposed to of flooded in 1885 they said the whole town was under water.

Is that right?

So I've heard, said the deputy.

I know it's burned down about a half a dozen times, said the storekeeper. You reckon there are just some places the good lord didn't intend folks to live in?

Could be, said the sheriff. He's got a bullheaded bunch to deal with here if it's so though, ain't he?

Damned if he don't.

Anything I can help ye with?

Naw, hell. We're tryin to salvage some of this stuff. I don't know. It sure is a hell of a mess.

Well. When you get those numbers let me have em. They'll most likely show up over in Knoxville.

I'd rather have the sons of bitches that stole em as have the guns back.

I know what you mean. We'll do our best.

Well.

Well, let me get my inboard cranked up here and we'll go pick up the mail.

The deputy grinned and dipped the oars into the gray water among the bottles and boards and floating fruit.

I'll talk to you later, Fate, said the storekeeper.

Okay Eustis. I hate it about your be in broke into.

Well.

They rowed on up the street and beached the skiff on the front steps of the post office and went in.

Mornin Sheriff Turner, said a pleasant woman from behind the barred window.

Mornin Mrs Walker, how you?

Wet. What about you?

Ain't this somethin?

She eased a bundle of mail beneath the bars.

This it?

That's it.

He leafed through the mail.

You ever find any of them people missin from them cars?

When we find one we'll find em all.

Well when are ye goin to find the one?

We'll find em.

I never knew such a place for meanness, the woman said.

The sheriff smiled. It used to be worse, he said.

Rowing back down Bruce Street they were hailed from an upper window. The sheriff leaned back to see who'd spoke, eyes squinted against the fine rain.

You goin to the courthouse, Fate?

Sure am.

How about a ride?

Come on.

Just let me get my coat I'll be right down.

An old man appeared at the top of a flight of stairs that ascended the side of a brick store building. He shut the door behind him and adjusted his hat and came down the steps with care. The deputy backed until the rear of the skiff came up against the stairs and the old man, taking a vicious grip on the sheriffs shoulder, stepped in and sat down.

Old woman told me today, said: It's a judgment. Wages of sin and all that. I told her everbody in Sevier County would have to be rotten to the core to warrant this. She may think they are, I don't know. How you, young feller?

Fine, said the deputy.

Here's a man can tell ye about the White Caps, said the sheriff.

People don't want to hear about that, said the old man.

Cotton here said it sounded like a good idea to him, the sheriff said. Keep people in line.

The old man studied the rowing deputy. Don't believe it, son, he said. They was a bunch of lowlife thieves and cowards and murderers. The only thing they ever done was to whip women and rob old people of their savins. Pensioners and widows. And murder people in their beds at night.

What about the Bluebills?

They was organized to set against the White Caps but they was just as cowardly. They'd hear the White Caps was ridin out someplace, like Pigeon Forge, they'd get out there and take up the boards in the bridge and lay in the bushes where they could hear em to fall through. They hunted one another all over the county for two year and never met but one time and that was by accident and in a narrow place where neither bunch couldn't run. No, those were sorry people all the way around, ever man jack a three hundred and sixty degree son of a bitch, which my daddy said meant they was a son of a bitch any way you looked at em.

What finally happened?

What finally happened was that one man with a little guts stood up to em and that was Tom Davis.

He was a wheelhorse wasn't he, Mr Wade.

He was that. He was just a deputy under Sheriff Millard Maples when he busted up the White Caps. He made three or four trips to Nashville, paid for it out of his own pocket. Got the legislature to pass a bill attaching the Circuit Court to the Criminal Court over in Knoxville so that they'd have a new judge in Sevierville and then he started after the White Caps. They tried ever way in the world to kill him. Even sicked a big nigger on him one night comin back from Knoxville. In them days you could go by steamboat and this nigger come off another boat in the middle of the river and pulled a gun to shoot him. Tom Davis took the gun away from him and just brought him on in to jail. By that time White Caps was leavin the county in droves. He didn't care where they went. He brought em back from Kentucky, from North Carolina, from Texas. He'd go off all by hisself and be gone weeks and come in with em on a string like a bunch of horses. He was the damnedest man I ever heard of. Was a educated man. Had been a school teacher. There had not been a Democrat elected in Sevier County since the Civil War, but when Tom Davis run for sheriff they elected him.

You don't remember the flood of 1885 do ye? said the deputy.

Well, bein as that was the year I was born my memory of it is somewhat dim.

What year was it they hung them two, Mr Wade.

That was in 99. That was Pleas Wynn and Catlett Tipton that had murdered the Whaleys. Got em up out of bed and blowed their heads off in front of their little daughter. They'd been in jail two years appealin and what not. There was a Bob Wade implicated in it too that I'm proud to report is no kin of mine. I think he went to the penitentiary. Tipton and Wynn, they hung them on the courthouse lawn right yonder.

157

It was right about the first of the year. I remember there was still holly boughs up and Christmas candles. Had a big scaffold set up had one door for the both of em to drop through. People had started in to town the evenin before. Slept in their wagons, a lot of em. Rolled out blankets on the courthouse lawn. Wherever. You couldn't get a meal in town, folks lined up three deep. Women sellin sandwiches in the street. Tom Davis was sheriff by then. He brung em from the jail, had two preachers with em and had their wives on their arms and all. Just like they was goin to church. All of em got up there on the scaffold and they sung and everbody fell in singin with em. Men all holdin their hats. I was thirteen year old but I remember it like it was yesterday. Whole town and half of Sevier County singin I Need Thee Every Hour. Then the preacher said a prayer and the wives kissed their husbands goodbye and stepped down off the scaffold and turned around to watch and the preacher come down and it got real quiet. And then that trap kicked open from under em and down they dropped and hung there a jerkin and a kickin for I don't know, ten, fifteen minutes. Don't ever think hangin is quick and merciful. It ain't. But that was the end of White Cappin in Sevier County. People don't like to talk about it to this day.

You think people was meaner then than they are now? the deputy said.

The old man was looking out at the flooded town. No, he said. I don't. I think people are the same from the day God first made one.

As they ascended the courthouse stairs he was telling them how an old hermit used to live out on House Mountain, a ragged gnome with kneelength hair who dressed in leaves and how people were used to going by his hole in the rocks and throwing in stones on a dare and calling to him to come out.

In the spring Ballard watched two hawks couple and drop, their wings upswept, soundless out of the sun to break and flare above the trees and ring up again with thin calls. He eyed them on, watching to see if one were hurt. He did not know how hawks mated but he knew that all things fought. He left the old wagonroad where it went through the gap and took a path that he himself kept, going across the face of the mountain to review the country that he'd once inhabited.

He sat with his back to a rock and soaked the warmth from it, the wind still cold that shivered the sparse high mountain bracken, the brittle gray ferns. He watched an empty wagon come up the valley below him, distant clatter of it, the mule pausing in the ford and the clatter of the immobile wagon rolling on regardless as if the sound authored the substance, until it had all reached his ears. He watched the mule drink and then the man on the wagonseat lifted one arm and they commenced again, now soundless, out of the creek and up the road and then again came the far muted wooden rumbling.

He watched the diminutive progress of all things in the valley, the gray fields coming up black and corded under the plow, the slow green occlusion that the trees were spreading. Squatting there he let his head drop between his knees and he began to cry.

LYING AWAKE in the dark of the cave he thought he heard a whistling as he used to when he was a boy in his bed in the dark and he'd hear his father on the road coming home whistling, a lonely piper, but the only sound was the stream where it ran down through the cavern to empty it may be in unknown seas at the center of the earth.

He dreamt that night that he rode through woods on a low ridge. Below him he could see deer in a meadow where the sun fell on the grass. The grass was still wet and the deer stood in it to their elbows. He could feel the spine of the mule rolling under him and he gripped the mule's barrel with his legs. Each leaf that brushed his face deepened his sadness and dread. Each leaf he passed he'd never pass again. They rode over his face like veils, already some yellow, their veins like slender bones where the sun shone through them. He had resolved himself to ride on for he could not turn back and the world that day was as lovely as any day that ever was and he was riding to his death.

ON A GOOD May morning John Greer turned out to dig a septic tank at the back of his house. While he was digging, Lester Ballard in frightwig and skirts stepped from behind the pumphouse and raised the rifle and cocked the hammer silently, holding back the trigger and easing it into the notch as hunters do.

When he fired the shovel was coming past Greer's shoulder with a load of dirt. Long after the crack of the rifle had died in the lee of the mountain he could hear the gong of turned doom that rang above the man's head as he froze there with the shovel aloft on which had splattered in a bright medallion the small piece of lead, the man looking at whatever it was standing there cursing to itself while it worked the lever of the rifle, an apparition created whole out of nothing and set upon him with such dire intent. He flung away the shovel and began to run. Ballard shot him through the body as he passed and stitched a falter in his pace. He shot him once more before he rounded the corner of the house but he could not tell where he hit him. He himself was running now, cursing steadily, working the lever of the rifle again, taking the corner of the house, one foot almost going from under him as he turned and making a vicious slash in the mud, the rifle now in one hand and his thumb hooked over the hammer, mounting the steps in a crazy sort of hopping gait and rushing toward the door.

He looked like something come against the end of a springloaded tether or some slapstick contrivance of the filmcutter's art, swallowed up in the door and discharged from it again almost simultaneously, ejected in an immense concussion backwards, spinning, one arm flying out in a peculiar limber gesture, a faint pink cloud of blood and shredded clothing and the rifle clattering soundless on the porchboards amid the uproar and Ballard sitting hard on the floor for a moment before he pitched off into the yard.

Even though Greer was shot through the upper chest himself he wobbled from the doorway with the shotgun and down the steps to examine this thing he'd shot. At the foot of the steps he picked up what appeared to be a wig and saw that it was fashioned whole from a dried human scalp.

BALLARD WOKE in a room dark to blackness.

He woke in a room day bright.

Woke in a room at dawn or dusk he knew not which where motes of dust passing through an unseen bar of light incandesced briefly and random and drifted like the smallest fireflies. He studied them for a while and then raised his hand. No hand came up. He raised the other and a thin stripe of yellow sunlight fell across his forearm. He looked about the room. Some stainless steel pots on a steel table. A pitcher of water and a glass. Ballard in a thin white gown in a thin white room, false acolyte or antiseptic felon, a practitioner of ghastliness, a part-time ghoul.

He had been awake for some few minutes before he began to feel about for the missing arm.

It was not in the bed at all.

He pulled the sheet from about his neck and studied the great swathings of bandage at his shoulder apparently with no surprise. He looked about. A room scarce wider than the bed. There was a small window behind him but he could not see out without craning his neck and it pained him to do so.

No one spoke to him. A nurse came with a tin tray and helped him to sit erect, Ballard still trying to use the missing arm to fetch his balance. A cup of soup, a cup of custard, a quarterpint of sweetmilk in a waxed cardboard box. Ballard prodded at the food with his spoon and lay back.

He lay in a waking dream. The cracks in the yellowed plaster of the ceiling and upper walls seemed to work on his brain. He could close his eyes and see them anyway. Thin fissures traversing the otherwise blank of his corroded mind. He looked at the swaddled nub that poked from the short sleeve of the county hospital gown. It looked like an enormous bandaged thumb. He wondered what they'd done with his arm and decided to ask.

When the nurse came with his supper he said: What'd they do with my arm?

She swung the tabletop and set the tray on it. You got it shot off, she said.

I know that. I just wanted to know what all they done with it.

I don't know.

It don't make a damn to you, does it?

No.

I'll find out. I can. Who's that feller at the door all the time?

He's a county deputy.

County deputy.

Yes, she said. What about the man you shot?

What about him?

Don't you even want to know if he's dead or alive?

Well.

He was unrolling his silver from the linen napkin.

Well what? she said.

Well is he dead or alive?

He's alive.

She watched him. He spooned up some applesauce and looked at it and put it down again. He opened the carton of milk and drank from it.

You really don't care one way or the other do you? she said.

Yes I do, said Ballard. I wish the son of a bitch was dead.

HE ATE, HE stared at the walls. He used the bedpan or chamberpot. Sometimes he could hear a radio in another room. One evening what appeared to be some hunters came to see him.

They talked for a while without the door. Then the door opened and the room filled up with men. They gathered about Ballard's bedside. He'd been asleep. He struggled up in the bed and looked at them. Some he knew, some not. His heart shrank.

Lester, said a heavyset man, where's them bodies at.

I don't know nothing about no bodies.

Yes you do. How many people did you kill?

I ain't killed nary'n.

The hell you ain't. You killed that Lane girl and burned her and that baby down in the house and you killed them people in them parked cars on the Frog Mountain.

I never done it.

They were quiet, regarding him. Then the man said: Get up, Lester.

Ballard pulled at the bedcovers. I ain't allowed up, he said.

A man reached and pulled back the covers. Ballard's spindly legs lay pale and yellow looking on the sheet.

Get up.

Ballard tugged at the hem of his nightgown to hide himself. He swung his legs over the side of the bed and sat there a minute. Then he stood up. He sat back down again and gripped the little table. Where we goin? he said.

Somebody in the back of the crowd said something but Ballard didn't catch it.

Is that all of a thing you got to wear?

I don't know.

They opened a closet and looked in but there were only some mops and a bucket. They stood there looking at Ballard. He didn't look like much.

We better get out of here if we're goin. Earl's likely gone to fetch the sheriff.

Let's go, Ballard.

They raised him up and pushed him toward the door and closed ranks behind him. He looked back once at the bed. Then they were going down the wide hospital corridor. Past open doors where people in bed watched him leaving, the linoleum cold under his feet and his legs wobbling a bit as he went.

It was a cool clear night. Ballard's eyes went upward to

the cold wash of stars that lay beyond the polelamps in the hospital parking lot. They crossed the black asphalt, damp from recent rain, and the men opened the door of a pickup truck and motioned Ballard in. He crawled up in the cab and sat with his bare legs together in front of him. Men got in on either side and the motor started and the lights came up and the lights from other cars and trucks down the parking lot. Ballard had to shift his knees like a child for the man to get to the gear lever. They pulled out of the parking lot and down the street.

Where we goin? said Ballard.

We'll all know when we get there, said the driver.

They drove out the highway toward the mountains, a caravan of trucks and cars. They stopped at a house. A man left the car behind Ballard and went to the door. A woman let him in. Inside under the glare of a naked bulb he could see the woman and some children. After a while the man came out again and came down to the truck and handed in a bundle through the window. Tell him put these here on, he said.

The driver handed the bundle to Ballard. Put them on, he said. It was a pair of overalls and an army shirt.

He sat in the truck with the clothes in his lap and they started on up the road again. They turned off onto a dirt road and wound through low hills with black pines sprocket-ing across the headlights in the curves and then they took another road, grass growing in it, coming at last out onto a high meadow where the remains of a sawmill stood in the starlight. A shed with the windows stoned lightless. Stacks of gray lumber, a sawdust pile where foxes lived.

The driver of the truck opened the door and stepped out. Other vehicles pulled alongside and men began to crowd about. A subdued sound of voices and cardoors closing. Ballard alone bareshank in his nightshift on the seat of the truck.

Let Otis watch him.

Why don't we just take him up here.

Let him set there.

How come he ain't put them clothes on.

The truck door opened. Ain't you cold, said a man.

Ballard looked at him dumbly. His arm hurt.

Tell him put them clothes on.

He wants you to put them there clothes on, the man said.

Ballard began to sort through the bundle for arm or leg holes.

Otis you watch him now.

Reckon we ort to tie his hands.

You could tie his hands to one of his legs like a mule.

Jerry you can put that jar right back where you got it from. This here is serious business.

Ballard had on the shirt and was trying to do the buttons. He'd never tried to button a shirt with one hand and he was not good at it. He got the overalls up and the straps fastened. They were soft and smelled of soap and there was room inside for a whole Ballard more. He tucked the loose sleeve of the shirt down inside the overalls and looked around. A man squatted in the bed of the truck with a shotgun watched him through the rear glass. Up on the hill by the sawmill a fire licked in the wind and the men were gathered around it. Ballard pushed the button on the glovebox door in front of him and it fell open. He felt among papers, found nothing. He shut the door again. After a while he cranked down the window.

You ain't got a cigarette back there have ye? he said.

The man leaned forward and held a pack of cigarettes up to the open window. Ballard took one and put it in his mouth. You got a match? he said.

The man handed him a match. How you fixed for spit? he said.

I never ast to come out here, said Ballard.

He popped the match on the dashboard and lit the cigarette and sat smoking in the dark, watching the fire on the hill. After a while a man came down and opened the door and told Ballard to get out. He climbed laboriously down and stood there in his overalls.

Bring him on up, Otis.

Ballard at gunpoint shuffling up the hill. He must pause to roll the cuffs of the overalls. At the fire he stood and looked down at his bare feet.

Ballard.

Ballard didn't answer.

Ballard, we're goin to let you make it light on yourself.

Ballard waited.

You show us where you put them people so they can be

give a decent burial and we'll put you back in that hospital and let you take your chances with the law.

You got it all, said Ballard.

Where's them bodies at, Ballard.

I don't know nothin about no bodies.

Is that your last say?

Ballard said that it was.

You got that cable, Fred?

Sure do.

A man stepped from the circle and came forward with a coiled and greasy braided steel cable.

You goin to have to tie that one arm down. Anybody got a rope in their truck?

I got one.

Ask him about that, Ernest.

Yeah Ernest.

The man turned to Ballard. What did you want with them dead ladies? he said. Was you fuckin em?

Ballard's face gave a funny little jerk in the firelight but he said nothing. He looked about at his tormentors. The man with the cable had uncoiled a part of it along the ground. There was a ring spliced into the end of it and the cable was pulled through in a loop like an enormous rabbit snare.

You know he was, the man said. Just take him on.

Someone was tying a rope about Ballard's arm. The steel cable slipped over his neck and rested on his shoulders. It was cold, smelled of oil.

Then he was walking up the hill toward the sawmill. They

173

helped him along, down the skids, stepping carefully, the flames from the bonfire stringing them in a ragged shadow-show across the upper hillside. Ballard slipped once and was caught up and helped on. They came to rest standing on an eight by eight above the sawdust pit. One of the men was boosted up to the overhead beams and handed up the slack end of the cable.

They ain't got him doped up have they, Ernest? I'd hate for him not to know what was happenin to him.

He looks alert enough to me.

Ballard craned his head toward the man who'd spoke. I'll tell ye, he said.

Tell us what?

Where they're at. Them bodies. You said if I'd tell you'd turn me loose.

Well you better get to telling.

They're in caves.

In caves.

I put em in caves.

Can you find em?

Yeah. I know where they're at.

BALLARD ENTERED the hollow rock that used to be his home attended by eight or ten men with lanterns and lights. The rest of them built a fire at the mouth of the cave and sat about to wait.

They gave him a flashlight and fell in behind him. Down

narrow dripping corridors, across stone rooms where fragile spires stood everywhere from the floor and a stream in its stone bed ran on in the sightless dark.

They went on hands and knees between shifted bedding planes and up a narrow gorge, Ballard pausing from time to time to adjust the cuffs of his overalls. His entourage somewhat in wonder.

You ever see anything to beat this?

We used to mess around in these old caves when I was a boy.

We did too but I never knowed about thisn here.

Abruptly Ballard stopped. Balancing with one arm, the flashlight in his teeth, he climbed a ledge and went along it with his face to the wall, went upward again, his bare toes gripping the rocks like an ape, and crawled through a narrow fissure in the stone.

They watched him go.

Goddamn if that there ain't a awful small hole.

What I'm thinkin is how we goin to get them bodies out of here if we do find em.

Well somebody shinny up there and let's go.

Here Ed. Hold the light.

The first man followed the ledge and climbed up to the hole. He turned sideways. He stooped.

Hand me that light up here.

What's the trouble?

Shit.

What is it?

175

Ballard!

Ballard's name faded in a diminishing series of shunted echoes down the hole where he had gone.

What is it, Tommy?

That little son of a bitch.

Where is he?

He's by god gone.

Well let's get after him.

I cain't get through the hole.

Well kiss my ass.

Who's the smallest?

Ed is, I reckon.

Come up here, Ed.

They boosted the next man up and he tried to wedge his way into the hole but he would not fit.

Can you see his light or anything?

Shit no, not a goddamn thing.

Somebody go get Jimmy. He can get through here.

They looked about at one another assembled there in the pale and sparring beams of their torches.

Well shit.

You thinkin what I am?

I sure as hell am. Does anybody remember how we came?

Oh fuck.

We better stick together.

You reckon there's another entrance to this hole he's in?

I don't know. You reckon we ought to leave somebody to watch here?

We might never find em again.

There's a lot of truth in that.

We could leave a light just around the corner here where it would look like somebody was a waitin.

Well.

Ballard!

Little son of a bitch.

Fuck that. Let's go.

Who wants to lead the way?

I think I can find it.

Well go ahead.

Goddamn if that little bastard ain't played us for a bunch of fools.

I guess he played em the way he seen em. I cain't wait to tell these boys outside what's happened.

Maybe we better odd man out to see who gets the fun of tellin em.

Watch your all's head.

You know what we've done don't ye?

Yeah. I know what we've done. We've rescued the little fucker from jail and turned him loose where he can murder folks again. That's what we've done.

That's exactly right.

We'll get him.

He may of got us. You remember this here?

I don't remember none of it. I'm just follerin the man in front of me.

FOR THREE DAYS Ballard explored the cave he'd entered in an attempt to find another exit. He thought it was a week and was amazed at how the batteries in the flashlight kept. He fell into the custom of napping and waking and going on again. He could find nothing but stone to sleep upon and his naps were brief.

Toward the end he would tap the flashlight against his leg to warm the dull orange glow of it. He took the batteries out and put them in again the hind one fore. Once he heard voices somewhere behind him and once he thought he saw a light. He made his way toward it in darkness lest it be the lights of his enemies but he found nothing. He knelt and drank from a dripping pool. He rested, drank again. He watched in the bore of his flashbeam tiny translucent fish whose bones in shadow through their frail mica sheathing traversed the shallow stonefloored pool. When he rose the water swung in his wasted paunch.

He scrabbled like a rat up a long slick mudslide and

entered a long room filled with bones. Ballard circled this ancient ossuary kicking at the ruins. The brown and pitted armatures of bison, elk. A jaguar's skull whose one remaining eyetooth he pried out and secured in the bib pocket of his overalls. That same day he came to a sheer drop and when he tried his failing beam it fell down a damp wall to terminate in nothingness and night. He found a stone and dropped it over the edge. It fell silently. Fell. In silence. Ballard had already turned to reach for another to drop when he heard far below the tiny spungg of the stone in water like a pebble down a well.

In the end he came to a small room with a thin shaft of actual daylight leaning in from the ceiling. It occurred to him only now that he might have passed other apertures to the upper world in the nighttime and not known it. He put his hand up into the crevice. He pried. He scratched at the dirt.

When he woke it was dark. He felt around and came up with the flashlight and pushed the button. A pale red wire lit within the bulb and slowly died. Ballard lay listening in the dark but the only sound he heard was his heart.

In the morning when the light in the fissure dimly marked him out this drowsing captive looked so inculpate in the fastness of his hollow stone you might have said he was half right who thought himself so grievous a case against the gods.

He worked all day, scratching at the hole with a piece of stone or with his bare hand. He'd sleep and work and sleep

179

again. Or sort among the dusty relics of a nest seeking a whole hickory nut among the bonehard hulls with their volute channels cleanly unmeated by woodmice, teeth precise and curved as sailmakers needles. He could find none, nor was he hungry. He slept again.

In the night he heard hounds and called to them but the enormous echo of his voice in the cavern filled him with fear and he would not call again. He heard the mice scurry in the dark. Perhaps they'd nest in his skull, spawn their tiny bald and mewling whelps in the lobed caverns where his brains had been. His bones polished clean as eggshells, centipedes sleeping in their marrowed flutes, his ribs curling slender and whitely like a bone flower in the dark stone bowl. He'd cause to wish and he did wish for some brute midwife to spald him from his rocky keep.

In the morning there was a spiderweb between himself and the sky. He seized a clawful of rubble and hurled it up the shaft. And again, until the web was gone every trace. He pulled himself up and began to dig.

He'd wake with his head against the wall and the stone tool still in his hand and dig again. Late that day he loosed a thin slab of stone and let it clatter down into the hole. In wrenching it loose he'd laid his finger open and he sat with it in his mouth, the earth's musty taste mingled with the ironrust tincture of blood. Dry dirt sifted down from the hole. He could see treelimbs against the sky.

Climbing up again he set to work, hammering now at actual stone, stratified layers of it that flaked off, Ballard using the larger chunks to pry and dig with. Before dark fell he raised his head up through the earth and looked out.

The first thing he saw was a cow. It was about a hundred feet away in a field beyond the wood in which he'd risen and beyond the cow was a barn and beyond that a house. He watched the house for signs of life but saw none. He lowered himself back into his hole and rested.

It was hours past dark and a black night when he finally emerged from the earth. Down at the house there were lights. He cast about among the stars for some kind of guidance but the heavens wore a different look that Ballard did not trust. He crossed through the woods and climbed a fence and crossed a field until he came to a road. It was no place he'd ever stood in before. Seeing that uphill it led toward the mountains he took the other way and soon was hobbling along weak but able, the night being as fine as you could wish and a faint bloom of honeysuckle already on the air. At this time he had not eaten for five days.

He'd not gone far before a churchbus hove into sight behind him. Ballard scuttled into the roadside weeds and crouched there watching. The bus clattered past. It was all lit up and the faces within passed each in their pane of glass, each in profile. At the last seat in the rear a small boy was looking out the window, his nose puttied against the glass. There was nothing out there to see but he was looking anyway. As he went by he looked at Ballard and Ballard looked back. Then the bus rounded the curve and clattered from sight. Ballard climbed into the road and went on. He was trying to fix in his mind where he'd seen the boy when it came to him that the boy looked like himself. This gave him the fidgets and though he tried to shake the image of the face in the glass it would not go.

When he reached the highway he crossed over into the fields beyond. He stumbled his way over the clods in a new turned bottom and came at last to the river. The river woods were hung with trash and papers from the high water, the trees plastered up with silt and enormous nests of jetsam lodged high in the branches against the sky.

As he neared the town the roosters were calling. Perhaps they sensed a relief in the obscurity of night that the traveler could not read, though he kept watch eastward. Perhaps some freshness in the air. Everywhere across the sleeping land they called and answered each to each. As in olden times so now. As in other countries here.

It was dawn when he presented himself at the county hospital desk. The nightduty nurse had just come down the hall with a cup of coffee and found Ballard leaning against the counter. A weedshaped onearmed human swaddled up in outsized overalls and covered all over with red mud. His eyes were caved and smoking. I'm supposed to be here, he said.

HE WAS NEVER indicted for any crime. He was sent to the state hospital at Knoxville and there placed in a cage next door but one to a demented gentleman who used to open folks' skulls and eat the brains inside with a spoon. Ballard saw him from time to time as they were taken out for airing but he had nothing to say to a crazy man and the crazy man had long since gone mute with the enormity of his crimes. The hasp of his metal door was secured with a bent spoon and Ballard once asked if it were the same spoon the crazy man had used to eat the brains with but he got no answer.

He contracted pneumonia in April of 1965 and was transferred to the University Hospital where he was treated and apparently recovered. He was returned to the state hospital at Lyons View and two mornings later was found dead in the floor of his cage.

His body was shipped to the state medical school at Memphis. There in a basement room he was preserved with formalin and wheeled forth to take his place with other

deceased persons newly arrived. He was laid out on a slab
and flayed, eviscerated, dissected. His head was sawed open
and the brains removed. His muscles were stripped from his
bones. His heart was taken out. His entrails were hauled
forth and delineated and the four young students who bent
over him like those haruspices of old perhaps saw monsters
worse to come in their configurations. At the end of three
months when the class was closed Ballard was scraped from
the table into a plastic bag and taken with others of his kind
to a cemetery outside the city and there interred. A minister
from the school read a simple service.

IN APRIL OF that same year a man named Arthur Ogle was plowing an upland field one evening when the plow was snatched from his hands. He looked in time to see his span of mules disappear into the earth taking the plow with them. He crawled with caution to the place where the ground had swallowed them but all was darkness there. A cool wind was coming from inside the earth and far below he could hear water running.

The following day two neighbor boys descended into the sink on ropes. They never found the mules. What they did find was a chamber in which the bodies of a number of people were arranged on stone ledges in attitudes of repose.

Late that afternoon the high sheriff of Sevier County with two deputies and two other men crossed the field from Willy Gibson's old rifle shop where they'd left the car and crossed the creek and went up the old log road. They carried lanterns and coils of rope and a number of muslin shrouds on which was stenciled Property of the State of Tennessee. The high sheriff of Sevier County himself descended into the sink and surveyed the mausoleum there. The bodies were covered with adipocere, a pale gray cheesy mold common to corpses in damp places, and scallops of light fungus grew along them as they do on logs rotting in the forest. The chamber was filled with a sour smell, a faint reek of ammonia. The sheriff and the deputy made a noose from a rope and they slipped it around the upper body of the first corpse and drew it tight. They pulled her from the slab and dragged her across the stone floor of the vault and down a corridor to where daylight fell against the wall of the sink. In this leaning bole of light, standing there among the shifting motes, they called for a rope. When it descended they made it fast to the rope about the corpse and called aloft again. The rope drew taut and the first of the dead sat up on the cave floor, the hands that hauled the rope above sorting the shadows like puppeteers. Gray soapy clots of matter fell from the cadaver's chin. She ascended dangling. She sloughed in the weem of the noose. A gray rheum dripped.

In the evening a jeep descended the log road towing a trailer in the bed of which lay seven bodies bound in muslin like enormous hams. As they went down the valley in the new fell dark basking nighthawks rose from the dust in the road before them with wild wings and eyes red as jewels in the headlights.